Hi Vickie
Rogers rocked!.
David~

Dave Kirendra
Jane Mensbroeker
"2011"

WITNESS THE TRUTH

Are You Being Deceived

Fredric Piepenbrok and
David Menebroeker

authorHOUSE®

AuthorHouse™
1663 Liberty Drive, Suite 200
Bloomington, IN 47403
www.authorhouse.com
Phone: 1-800-839-8640

First published by AuthorHouse 12/12/2008

ISBN: 978-1-4389-2024-5 (sc)

Library of Congress Control Number: 2008908819

Printed in the United States of America
Bloomington, Indiana

This book is printed on acid-free paper.

FORWARD

Our hope is that this book will bring to light the true words of God in this age of satanic darkness. It has been written to bring us closer to our Father through the exposing of satan and his lies.

Its truth should hopefully bring us to love, honor, and respect Him just as His Son Yeshua, His Christ and our Savior did, as well as those of the early Christian church.

Theirs was a total obedience, even unto death, setting the example for us to follow.

Our hope is also that this work will open your eyes and ears to His wisdom, knowledge, and understanding to give witness and testimony in that evil day to come, thereby fulfilling God's plan for us and all who would obey.

CONTENTS

INTRODUCTION

The purpose of this book is to help those who want to dig deeper into Gods' Truth through the exposing of satan, and the questioning of the status quo, and the present day teachings, or the lack of them. Satan would rather you didn't question any of what is taught today as biblical truth because then he would be disclosed for what he really is, a liar. Sorry to say but there are many people, who through pride and willful ignorance, unknowingly support satan's deceptions through their comfortable habits, traditions, and teachings.

God, on the other hand, has always stood for Truth and has it written for all to see, if we have ears to hear and eyes to see. What that means is, we have to dig into what in fact really is written, and search through the smoke and mirrors to know clearly His words and purpose in our lives. It's not always comfortable and, as soon as you get a handle on the Truth, someone else will definitely become offended by it. Why? It makes them uncomfortable too (Luke12:51-53).

Christ speaking to those who would refuse to believe in Him says in John 8:44; "You are of your father the devil, and the desires of your father you want to do. He was a murderer from the beginning, and does not stand in the truth, because there is no truth in him. When he speaks a lie, he speaks from his own resources, for he is a liar and the father of it." He was addressing the church leaders who were comfortable in a lie. So who do you want the Christ to say your father is?

Satan is also described in the Bible as the deceiver of the whole world in Rev 12:9; "So the great dragon was cast out, that old serpent of old, called the Devil and Satan, who deceives the whole world, he was cast to the earth, and his angels were cast with him." With that in mind, doesn't it stand to reason that there would be many false doctrines and ideas, as well as worship practices, in our world? If you doubt that, then just browse any book of the world's major religions, let alone all the minor ones. Confusion and chaos will definitely come to mind as you try to summarize them collectively. Satan's deception is well ingrained in our world but it can in fact be ferreted out with an open mind and a little research.

Paul says that satan transforms himself into a minister of light and righteousness, as do those that follow him in 2 Cor11:12-14; "But what I do, I will also continue to do, that I may cut off the opportunity from those who desire an opportunity to be regarded just as we are in the things of which they boast. For such are false apostles, deceitful workers, transforming themselves into apostles of Christ. And no wonder! For satan himself transforms himself into an angel of light." So now just from that alone, wouldn't you expect to see his deception in the churches and religions of this present world, with Christianity and your church being no exception? If you're already uncomfortable or offended ask yourself why? The money changers of the temple didn't want their boat rocked either but it had to be done to fulfill the Fathers plan.

Satan is described as the adversary of mankind in 1Peter 5:8; "Be sober, be vigilant, because your adversary (Gk. = "Antidikos" = an opponent as the arch enemy) the devil walks about like a roaring lion, seeking whom he may devour." If this is the case, then he is the arch enemy against Truth, so wouldn't it be wise to check into what we call truth so as not to become devoured? When Paul took the Truth to the Bereans, it is said of them in Acts

17:11; "These were more fair-minded than those in Thessalonica, in that they searched the Scriptures daily to find out whether these things were so". Wouldn't you think that this was written so that we too, in this age, might be as diligent and take the time to question and check into our premise through Scripture?

It would seem especially important once we remember that Christ states in Matt 7:13; "Enter by the narrow gate; for wide is the gate and broad is the way that leads to destruction, and there are many who go in by it." Then wouldn't it seem wise to make sure that we were not one of those many on that broad path to destruction? Just from this one scriptural idea alone you can pretty much be assured, that if there is a universal acceptance of a practice or idea, that it is in all probability not in line with Gods teachings but is really just a part of that broad way to destruction. Do you really believe that the mainstream movement of this world, whether political, economic, educational, or religious, is taking the world somewhere good? History says no! If someone is selling a million books, or there is a popular movement, or new idea that is sure to bring peace and prosperity, you can be sure it is really only good for the one touting the idea. The masses will usually suffer through fleecing, greater confusion, prejudicial domination or worse murder, theft, rape, and destruction.

1 Thess 5:21 says to "Test (prove in the King James) all things; hold fast what is good." Our Father's Truth is the only sure thing we will ever have, and so we need to anchor or hold fast to it, to withstand the storms of life's turbulent seas.

Having established that satan is a liar, and the father of them, then we must also recognize his supreme desire in lying. It is stated in Matt 4:9 and again in Luke 4:7; "Therefore, if you will worship me, all will be yours." He wants desperately to be worshiped! So much so that he will give everything to attain that worship. He wants to be in the seat of the Father. Isaiah 14:13 confirms it where satan says he will "exalt my (satan's) throne above the stars of God;" because as stated in Ezk 28:17; "Your (satan's) heart was lifted up because of your (satan's) beauty."

We need to be smart enough to recognize him when he (satan) "...sits as God in the temple of God, showing himself that he is God" (2 Thess 2:4). And just where is the temple of God? 1 Cor 3:16; "Do you not know that you are the temple of God and that the Spirit of God dwells in you? If it is a deceiving spirit that you choose to follow then that spirit is in fact your indwelling god just as satan wants it. It gets kind of personal doesn't it?

Satan is part of a plan and purpose being worked out here on earth and each of us has a part in it. Satan's role, from our perspective, is second only to God's as he is also described as the god of this world age in 2 Cor 4:3-4; "But even if our gospel is veiled to those who are perishing, whose minds the <u>god of this age</u> has blinded, who do not believe, lest the light of the gospel of the glory of Christ, who is the image of God, should shine on them."

They are the power and we are the pawns, but pawns with a personal choice as to which power we will be subject to. God the Father is the supreme power with the Christ being our salvation and the way to that Father, but God has also allowed satan temporary domination to test and prove our true will. In Deut 30:19 God says; "I call heaven and earth as witness today against you, that I have set before you life and death, blessing and cursing, therefore choose life, that both you and your descendants may live."

There is only one true God and that is the Father, and the way to Him is through His Christ. They are that life that is set before us. Satan and his lies, children, and deceptions are the other choice and it leads us to the death that is also set before us.

Our hope is that through this eye opening book, and your choice, you will be one who God can say "well done, good and faithful servant, you have been faithful over a few things, I will make you ruler over many things. Enter into the joy of your Lord." (Matt 25:23)

CHAPTER 1

How to Study the Bible

The first thing is to understand what the Bible is. Some list it as an old and not so reliable history. Some would say it is an out of date book and others say it is good for teaching some things, but not pertinent to everything. Some say the old covenant is just a historical record and the new is all that pertains. But what does the Bible say about itself? First, it puts the strictest of all proofs upon itself by stating that "<u>all</u> Scripture is given by inspiration of God, and is profitable for doctrine, for reproof, for correction, for instruction in righteousness, that the man of God may be complete, thoroughly equipped for every good work" (2 Tim 3:16). In other words it is all right or it is all wrong! There is no room for error or God is not in fact God, as He alone is deemed infallible. No other book in the world can make such a claim and stick by it. No other book in the world has been subject to such scrutiny and stood the test.

We also need to address what Paul states in Eph 2:19-22 when he says; "Now, therefore, you are no longer strangers and foreigners, but fellow citizens with the saints and members of the household of God, having been built on the foundation of the apostles and prophets, Jesus Christ Himself being the chief cornerstone, in whom the whole building, being joined together, grows into a holy temple in the Lord, in whom you also are being built together for a dwelling place of God in the Spirit." We need to take notice of this foundation. The apostles wrote and represent the New Testament, and the prophets wrote and represent the Old Testament, with Yeshua (the Christ's spoken name meaning God's salvation, with Christ being a title of the messiah, and Jesus being a corruption of the Greek word "Lesous") being the cornerstone where they meet and come together. As the Bible itself says all scripture is pertinent.

The Bible we normally see today is generally broken into an old and a new testament and this causes misunderstanding in its usage. The tribe of Judah was given the blessing of the scepter (the symbol of the kingly line) and is the keeper of the Books, or Torah, or Law (Gen 49:10), and even the

Quran acknowledges this fact. The language of the Jew and the Law is Hebrew and the Tanakh (Old Testament) is a "B'rit" or covenant (a contract). The "B'rit Hadassah" (New Testament) is also a covenant, but written in Greek, and the word for "B'rit" in Greek is "Diatheke".

The problem is that the Greek word can also be translated "testament" in English whereas the Hebrew can not. The trouble comes in that a testament is a written instruction telling what to do with someone's property after ones death. It is not the same as the original contract definition. You can't have two valid testaments but you can have two valid contracts. Since all Scripture is pertinent you need to see them as what they are, not what they are not. They are both covenants. The "old" is not "bad" either but only earlier in the sense of time. Nevertheless the two covenants form one Bible and the two parts deal with parallel material in a complimentary way. Thus the New Testament apart from the Old is heretical and the Old Testament apart from the New is incomplete. Two Covenants, (Testaments) one Bible.

In ancient books we look for more than one copy to authenticate the work. Most either stand alone, and so become more subject to criticism, or have one or two copies so that they can be relied upon as to their own genuine stature. If you were to have a work of say Homer or Socrates you would consider it accurate or genuine if you had another copy to compare it to, or at least had other works that made supportive reference to it. Our numbers may be off some but the argument for scriptural accuracy becomes a mute point in that the most copies of any ancient work not even close to the age of the Bible is not much more than seven, with one or two being the norm. Many stand alone. Make the number doubled or fourteen copies. Wouldn't you say you had a pretty accurate and valid copy? The Bible has over twenty thousand references and fragments. Cut it in half, and in half again for errors sake, and you can still see that what we have is an over abundance of Biblical writings that check and recheck themselves.

Cynics have tried over the centuries to disprove the Bible, especially historically, but dig after archeological dig has always proven it to be correct and not otherwise. If you think it was just written by man without inspiration then explain the numerical structure and mathematical phenomena inherent to it and found everywhere in it's pages. It was written by forty-two different men over a time span of some fourteen hundred years and yet it has been found that while one out of every five scriptures in the Bible contains a number that even the numbers themselves, as well as their numerical occurrence, is consistently structured throughout the whole Word. There is a whole book dedicated to this theme and is quite fascinating in itself titled <u>Biblical Mathematics Keys to Scripture Numerics</u> by Vallowe. The phenomena is also listed and referred to in <u>The Companion Bible</u> by Kregel Publications.

If that weren't enough, then there are the fulfilled prophesies that are written seven hundred to a thousand years before the fact and yet history itself proves them all to be accurate. We can't even get the weather predicted for more than a couple of days and even that is iffy. The mathematical odds against Christ fulfilling the hundreds of prophesies about his person are ten to the astronomical number to one and yet He hits the proverbial nail every time.

If you're still not appreciative of the remarkable uniqueness of the Bible then all you have to do is look to the heavens themselves. The Zodiac, which is older than any writings of man and universal to all cultures, depicts the plan of God for mankind. It has corruption now to be sure, as it has come down to us from antiquity, but a study of the ancient names of stars and major and minor constellations follows the course of history and Biblical prophesies as well. There are two books that cover that study well called <u>The Glory of the Stars</u> by E. Raymond Capt and <u>The Witness of the Stars</u> by E. W. Bullinger. Is it any real wonder that the creator of the heavens uses the very stars themselves, through naming and placement, to support the Bible and its message to mankind?

Perhaps the best proof of all is to just read the entire Bible and see how it pertains to your life and answers your questions. To be sure it will bring up more questions, some of which may be answered here among these pages, and some will linger for years. The end result however is that it is a unique and living work that stands alone and stands the test of time and cynics alike.

It should also be stated that, when studied, we must remember that the context must be considered as well as making a distinction of the subject and the verb. For example, one of the most frequent and common mistakes made in Biblical consideration is the substitution of Judah for Israel. Jews are one thirteenth of the whole and the fact that the present day Jew lives in a country called Israel doesn't change that. God certainly knows who is who and so should we if we are to correctly interpret scripture.

Then too, there is a thread of continuum that weaves itself through the pages of Biblical thought. There is a constant reference to both the physical meaning as well as the spiritual. There are the present time and people, the future, and the past to be considered. You can't put God in a box nor His Word. They just don't fit. If something doesn't make sense then consider the size of your box. The larger picture of God probably needs expansion.

In 1 Cor 10 Paul speaking of the ancient Israelites says in verse 11; "Now these things happened to them as examples, and they were written for our admonition, on whom the end of the ages (world in the King James = "Aion" in the Greek = an age, specifically a messianic period, <u>not the end of a Jewish period</u>) have come. If past, present, and future are not considered then you're cutting yourself short as well as that thread of continuum. How else would the thought of Eccl 1:9 make sense when it states; "That which has been is what will be, that which is done is what will be done, and there is nothing new under the sun." Why you could almost read the Bible backwards to find out the future.

Matthew 20:16 is another example where multiple thought is conveyed; "So the last will be first, and the first will be last. For many are called, but few chosen." Considering physical time and spiritual condition will paint a more complete picture here. Ezek 12:2 says; "Son of man, you dwell in the midst of a rebellious house, which has eyes to see but does not see, and ears to hear but does not hear, for they are a rebellious house." Romans 11:7-8 repeat that thought but injects the elect as having the eyes and ears. So here we need to ask which house? We need to consider the past house, the present house, the spiritual house, and the physical one. Remember too that the Jew of today is not all of Israel.

John 6:44 claims, "No one can come to Me (Yeshua) unless the Father (Yahweh) who sent Me draws him, and I will raise him up on the last day." The question to be asked then is; Has He drawn you and do you have eyes to see and ears to hear or are you part of that rebellious house? A study on eyes and ears, in itself, would be eye opening to be sure.

There are many translations of the Bible but fortunately we also have books such as <u>Strong's Exhaustive Concordance of the Bible</u> and also <u>Thayer's</u> that take each word of the Bible back to its original language for unsurpassed clarity of original thought. The original work of the Bible is authenticated, but the various translations are made with doctrinal and prejudicial additions and omissions. Some error is unintentional for sure, but it's still there none the less. Thankfully, with the help of those references mentioned, when the original language is referred to, the thought intended is then made clearer.

For example; Rom 10:4 is usually quoted to show that God's law is done away with as it states that; "Christ is the end of the law for righteousness to everyone who believes." Sounds right doesn't it? But Matt 5:18 says; "For assuredly, I say to you, till heaven and earth pass away, one jot or one tittle will by no means pass from the law till all is fulfilled." Christ Himself says in Matt 5:17; "Do not think that I came to destroy the Law or the Prophets. I did not come to destroy but to fulfill." Now if all Scripture is good for reproof and doctrine as stated in 2 Tim 3:16 then we have a problem, as these thoughts are contradictory. One scripture seems to say the Law is finished and two seem to say it is not. When we look up the word for "end" in the contradictory verse we find the Greek word "Telos". It is where we get our English word for telescope. It means the point aimed at, or the zenith, or culmination. Now to culminate and terminate are both synonymous with the English word end but the difference in thought is profound. All Law culminates or points to Christ, not end or terminate in Him. Considered properly, as such, all three verses are harmonious and, in fact, witness to each other in that harmony.

Even plain logic will help in solving the matter if a cloven hoof is digging in to fight the thought purification. If God wanted to do away with the Law, and everything that today calls "Jewish", then

He obviously made a big mistake in the first place. Then too, why would He send the Christ as a Torah observant Jew and not a gentile? Either today's "Christians" are wrong or God is. Which would you bet on if your life depended on it (and it does) to be true?

If, by the way, you want to know what was nailed to the cross with Yeshua look to Eph 2:15 where it says; "… having abolished in His flesh the enmity, that is, the law of commandments <u>contained in ordinances,</u> so as to create in Himself one new man from the two, thus making peace." The blood sacrifices were the handwriting of requirements, or ordinances, that were wiped out not the whole Torah or Law. Hebrews 7:27 confirms that thought where it says; "For this He did once for all when He offered up Himself." In other words, His one blood sacrifice makes continuous animal sacrifice unnecessary.

There are many more erroneous word and thought translations throughout the various versions of the Bible, as we shall see as we proceed with our work here. For purposes of this book the New King James will be referred to or the King James if so noted.

CHAPTER 2

How Old is the Earth?

The query of the earth's age has led to some of the greatest criticism of Christianity and rightly so. It being only six thousand years old has been adhered to by many for some time now. The use of a day for a thousand years, as found in 2 Peter 3:8 is applied, but in fact no where in that passage is the creation itself pointed to. It is true that it is very hard to come up with a historical document that predates that time period of six thousand years. The stone it was written on may be more ancient but when it was written is another point. And so the argument goes. But what has Christianity got to say about the fossil record and the dating of them? To be sure, our scientists might be, and have been, off by tens of thousands of years but there are still tens of thousands of years or more to be reckoned with.

While scientists dig in the ground, Christians dig in their heels but that won't correct the error.

What does God, in the Bible, say? Gen 1:1 "In the beginning God created the heavens and the earth." It does not say when the beginning was just that God created it. The word for God is interesting too. The Father's name is the four Hebrew lettersYud-Hey-Vav-Heh as given in Ex 6:3 and again in Ex 15:3, as well as the shortened Eh-Yeh in Ex 3:14. It is usually pronounce Yahweh with Adonai or HaShem substituted by the Israelites to avoid mispronouncing the sacred name whose vowel sounds have been lost due to non-use over the centuries. But the word used in the Gen 1:1 creation story is "Elohiym", which is a pluralistic sense of God, or Gods.

To help us understand this, look to Col 1:15-16 where it speaks of Yeshua saying; "He is the image of the invisible God, the firstborn over all creation." "Firstborn" is the Greek word "Protokos" which means to bear, or born, delivered, chief of all, or foremost of all creation. This scripture alone separates Him from the Father more than any other but there are more that bear witness to the same thought. Mark 13:32; "But of the day and hour no one knows, not even the angels in heaven, nor the Son, but <u>only the Father</u>." Yeshua Himself says in Luke 22:42; "...not My will, but

Yours, be done." John 8:28 Yeshua states; "...I do nothing of myself but as My Father taught Me." Col 1:16 then goes on to say; "for by Him all things were created that are in heaven and that are on the earth, visible and invisible, whether thrones or dominions or principalities, or powers. All things were created through Him and for Him." Do you now comprehend the separation of the Father and the Son so that they can say we and not I? They are not one God, and so "Elohiyim" is used as a family name to describe them.

John 1:1-2 states; "In the beginning was the Word, and the Word was God. He was in the beginning <u>with</u> God." Verse 14 goes on; "And the Word became flesh and dwelt among us, and we beheld His glory as the only begotten of the Father, full of grace and truth." Eph 3:9 shows the plurality for the creation too where it says; "...in God who created all things through Jesus Christ." Genesis:1 goes on with that same pattern in the later verse 26 saying;"...Let <u>us</u> make man in <u>our</u> image..." So now we can see that the Bible makes it very clear that both the Father and the Son were present as "Elohiym" in the creation process.

Obviously one word can truly mean a lot, so let's go on with the time sequence. Verse two of Genesis one goes on to say; "The earth was without form, and void, and darkness was upon the face of the deep. And the spirit of God was hovering over the face of the waters." The Hebrew word for without form is "Tohuw" and the word for void is "Bohuw". "Tohuw" translates a confusion, to lay waste, a worthless thing, in vain and empty or a place of chaos. "Bohuw" means an undistinguishable ruin or emptiness. The word used for "darkness" is "Choshek" and it translates darkness, misery, destruction, and death, wickedness and sorrow. When we truly contemplate the meaning of these words then we, once again, have a scriptural contradiction.

The problem lies with 1Cor 14:33. It says; "For God is <u>not</u> the author of confusion but of peace, as in all the churches of the saints." God then is either the author of confusion and chaos or not, depending on which scripture you want to refer to. There are, however, more scriptures that witness to the fact that He is not. Job 38:4 asks; "Where were you when I laid the foundations of the earth… and verse 7 goes on; "When the morning stars sang together and all the sons of God shouted for joy?" Would you shout for joy over void and waste? And then too Isaiah 45:18 reads; "For thus says the Lord, who created the heavens, who is God, who formed the earth and made it, who established it, <u>who did not create it in vain</u>, who formed it to be inhabited: I am the Lord, and there is no other." The word for vain used here is the same Hebrew word "Tohuw" used in Gen1:2.

The problem with the contradictory scripture is remedied when the single word used to translate "was" is considered. The word is "Hayah" and it means to exist, be, or become, and come to pass. It is translated to come to pass, or became, in over a hundred places in the first two books alone. If you read it thus, the translation then agrees with the rest of Scripture. "In the beginning God created the heavens and the earth. The earth became without form, and void; and darkness was upon the face of the deep". The earth was created not in confusion but in the perfection of Yahweh and Yeshua, so that the sons of God had reason to shout for joy, but it became void and waste and covered with water and darkness.

How and why it became that way is answered by looking into the author of confusion himself. James 3:14-16; "But if you have bitter envy and self-seeking in your hearts do not boast and lie against the truth. This wisdom does not descend from above, but is earthly, sensual, <u>demonic</u>. For where envy and self-seeking exist, <u>confusion and every evil</u> thing are there." So, according to Scripture, confusion is of the devil. It also states in Ezek 28:15 of satan; "You were perfect in your ways from the day you were created, till iniquity (Heb. = "Evel" =

evil, iniquity, perverseness) was found in you. Verse 16; "…Therefore I cast you out of the mountain of God; …verse 17; "I cast you to the ground" (Heb. = "Erets" = the earth). The same is similarly repeated in Isaiah 14. The summation of it all is, that when satan was cast out of heaven and to the earth, that was what caused it to become darkness, evil, emptiness, chaos, waste, and ruin, not only on the earth then, but in our very lives now.

Now we can see that Elohiym initially created the earth in perfection and to be inhabited. It then became a void and waste when satan tried to ascend to the throne of God, starting a great war in heaven. This is the first earth age spoken of in 2Peter 3:5-7; "For this they willfully forget that by the word of God the heavens were of old, and the earth standing out of the water and in the water, by which the world that then existed perished, being flooded with water. This is where we get our fossil record and probably even our 23 ½ degree tilt. The destruction was not a gradual process, and neither was the formation of the Grand Canyon, as modern research has shown. There are, in fact, still mastodons frozen so fast up in Alaska that they still have buttercups (Not a flower of the cold) in their mouths. The meat is still good enough to be fed to sled dogs. No this was an act of great upheaval, that throwing down of satan. The ancient dinosaurs are a real life fact and the first earth age is too.

The argument from some will be that the flood of Noah caused all that, but again we need to look at all the facts and ask questions that demand answers. The flood of Noah can be traced from Adaam and his descendants to the year 2345 on 1 November. This is also confirmed through careful analysis of Chinese, Babylonian, Hebrew, Mexican, Peruvian, and Egyptian records. Books that can give light to the subject are <u>Tracing our Ancestors</u> by Frederick Haberman and the <u>Great Pyramid Its Devine Message</u> by D. Davidson and H. Aldersmith, and <u>The Phoenician Origin of Britons and Scots and Anglo Saxons</u> Discovered by Phoenician and Sumerian Inscriptions in Briton by Pre Roman Briton Coins by Waddell as well as <u>Miracle of the Ages</u> by Worth Smith.

The Egyptian Sed Festivals, or dynasties, were continuous and are documented as continuing through the flood time period of Noah. They knew nothing of the flood of Noah until the building of the great pyramid of Gizeh where the flood is then recorded in their <u>Book of the Dead</u>. That pyramid was built beginning around 2200 b.c.e. a couple of hundred years after the flood and finished around 2170 b.c.e. and yet they were able to supply a work force of upward of 100,000 men rotating in relays of three months each. Eight souls could not have multiplied to that extent in that amount of time.

More proofs than that are added when the Chinese <u>Shu King</u> book is referred to. The Chinese Dynasties also reigned throughout the time period of Noah's flood and even lists the forty cities that were destroyed when its waters receded from the Pamir Plateau area. It then goes on to describe Noah as "FuHi", a man with a rainbow about him. The native peoples of Turkistan still speak of the wood that was taken from the ark to make pendants that were claimed to give a blessing to them.

If all this still leaves you with your traditional heals dug in then go to the Bible itself. The Fenton translation of the Bible in Gen 10:5 says of Noah's sons; "From these they spread themselves over the seacoasts of the countries of the nations, each with their language <u>among the gentile</u> (heathen) <u>tribes</u>." Verses 31 and 32; "These are the sons of Shem, by their tribes and by their languages in their countries <u>among the heathen</u>. The above were the families of the sons of Noah, and their descendants by tribes. From them <u>they spread themselves among the nations on the earth after the flood</u>." By looking up the original language of Hebrew you can see that this Fenton translation is an accurate one.

Other works that have addressed this same topic call the time from "in the beginning" to "it became void and waste" the gap theory, but I think we can see it is more a Biblical fact than a theory and is backed by outside scientific, as well as historical, analysis of the earth's ancient age.

CHAPTER 3

How Old is Mankind?

Scientists say man is ancient and Christians say six thousand years. Which is right? Actually both as we shall see from the scriptures themselves. Gen 1:26; "Let us make man in our image" (once again confirming the plurality of "Elohiym"). The word for man uses the Hebrew word "Aadaam", meaning man or mankind. Then in Gen 2:4 it states; "This is the history (or generations in the King James) of the heavens and the earth…" and then in verse 7 it says; "And the Lord God (Yahweh Elohiym) formed man (Hebrew = "Et Ha Aadaam") of the dust of the ground and breathed into his nostrils the breath of life and man (once again "Haa Aadaam") became a living being.

The use of the article and particle "Et Ha" denotes this particular one out of the whole. "Et" and the

"Ha" is a demonstration of emphatic division. This particular man out of mankind, and absolutely no other, was made for the seed line to the Christ and to till the ground, and no other was so chosen, or formed, or able. That seed line to the Christ was why satan came so fast to disrupt and corrupt that particular man and his seed line but, thankfully, to no real avail.

This also gives answer to the question as to why Cain was marked. So the other people ("Aadaam") would be distinguished from him. Eve's oldest son went as a marked man, among mankind, to the east of Eden in the land of Nod. There he married and built cities and taught dragon worship which is still prevalent there. The ShuKing books, or writings, of China confirm it.

Now it can be seen through the original biblical language that mankind ("Aadaam") was made before that particular man we commonly call Adam ("Et Ha Aadaam"). If you look into the ancient people's records you will find that mankind ("Aadaam") suddenly flourishes with knowledge when contacted and taught by the noble race of Adam's ("Et HA Aadaam's") children. The Egyptian records are some of the most notable, and best documented, and <u>Miracle of the Ages</u> by Worth Smith is one of the books to summarize the information. <u>Stonehenge and Druidism</u> by Capt ties the same teaching and building phenomena of Egypt to ancient Britain's monuments.

The Et Ha Adamic people, long ago, took the plan of God to all the corners of the earth. There is indeed "nothing new under the sun". Even the Seminole people of Florida, when contacted by Europeans in the fifteenth century, were expecting a fair skinned savior. Sorry to say the Spanish Catholic and English and French Protestants were not that savior, nor did they represent Him very well, as American history has shown. A look into Phoenician origin and history will shed further light on the subject. Willful ignorance becomes the only alibi after all sources, including the Bible and just plain logic, are considered. "Aadaam" is older than the six thousand years of "Et Ha Aadaam".

CHAPTER 4

Wheat and Tares

There are several references by Yeshua the Christ as to the tares that are here in this age, but the most significant is in Matt 13:36-40. It says; "Then Jesus sent the multitude away and went into the house. And His disciples came to Him, saying; "Explain to us the parable of the tares of the field." He answered and said to them; "He who sows the good seed is the Son of Man. The field is the world, the good seed are the sons of the kingdom, but the tares are the sons of the wicked one. The enemy who sowed them is the devil, the harvest is the end of the age (this earth age) and the reapers are the angels. Therefore as the tares are gathered and burned in the fire, so it will be at the end of this age" (earth age).

Greek uses the word "Sopros" when referring to the seed of plants as in Mark 4:26 and "Sperma" when referring to the seed of man as in Luke 1:55. In the above context of Matt 13 the word used is "Sperma".

If we go back to Gen 3:13 in the Garden of Eden it says; "And the LORD God (Yahweh Elohiym, which would be the Father) said to the woman, what is this that you have done? The woman said, the serpent deceived me, and I ate." Now this is where preachers start to say that Eve ate of an apple from a tree and so sinned. Did you see anything of an apple tree mentioned? Look all you want and there will not be found even a hint of one. But look to the Hebrew word used for "deceived". It is "Nasha" and it can mean beguiled or deceived, but also to seduce or steal the heart away but in the sense of utterly seducing. Then too in verse seven their eyes were opened and they knew they were naked, and sewed fig leaves together and made coverings. The word for covering is "Chagorot" and means a loin cloth or apron so we all know what it was they were covering in their new found nakedness. If that isn't enough then we are told that Eve's punishment is to bear children in pain. It starts to look kind of sexual doesn't it?

Before you pass judgment look to the New Testament in 2 Cor 11:3 where Paul says;"But I fear, lest somehow, as the serpent deceived (beguiled in the King James) Eve by his craftiness, so your minds may be corrupted from the simplicity that is in Christ". The Greek word for deceived or beguiled is "Expatao" and it means to wholly, totally seduce. And what is the outcome? Gen 4; She bears and bears again. The Hebrew word is "Watacep" and means a continuation of the bearing. She had twins! You can also know that by the fact that they both came of age for sacrificing at the same time. But now ask yourself why Cain is not listed in the lineage of Et Ha Aadaam? Cain's line is listed in Gen. Chapter 4, while Adaam's is listed separately in Chapter 5. And why are they separate?

It becomes more clear when both John the Baptist and Yeshua the Christ call the Scribes and Pharisees for what they really are, a brood of vipers. They, like satan, are filled with the same attributes and ascribe to the same high seats as satan, all the while claiming to be righteous. John 8:44 makes it perfectly clear when Yeshua answers them by stating "You are of your father the devil, and the desires of your father you want to do".

The seed line through Cain (Kennites) is with us to the end of the age. This is reinforced in Matt13:30; "Let both (wheat and tares) grow together until the harvest and at the time of the harvest I will say to the reapers, First gather together the tares and bind them in bundles to burn them, but gather the wheat into my barn." The Greek word for tares is "Zizania" a darnel or zowan that looks just like wheat when it grows but when it comes to fruitation it has a black, useless, seed that is good for nothing. Is it any wonder that "every tree is known by its fruit" (Luke 6:44)? A word study on fruit will also bear this whole theme out.

Remember the aprons of fig leaves and not apple leaves? Well it's interesting that there are two kinds of figs also; a Shmyrna which is feminine and bears good edible fruit and a male Capri which bears a bad and inedible fruit. They are both mentioned in Jer 24. There were also two trees in the Garden of Eden which were not to be taken of. The tree of Life (Christ) and the tree of the knowledge of good and evil (satan). You see the two seed lines and the two choices are still here before us. Is it any wonder that it says to us in Matt 24:32; "Now learn the parable of the fig tree:" A study of the fig tree and its symbolism along with fruit as used throughout the Bible is an interesting study indeed.

CHAPTER 5

The First Big Lie

Genesis 3:4 is the first of satan's lies that is recorded and states: "...You will surely not die" but in fact we not only do but the Bible states;

Ps 6:5; "For in death there is no remembrance of You: in the grave who will give thanks."

Ps 30:9; "What profit is there in my blood, when I go down to the pit? Will the dust praise You?"

Ps 115:17; "The dead do not praise the Lord; nor any who go down in silence."

Ps 49:12; "Nevertheless man, though in honor, does not remain (endure); He is like the beasts that perish."

⇥ *Fredric Piepenbrok and David Menebroeker* ⇤

Ps 143:3; "For the enemy has persecuted my soul; He has crushed my life to the ground; (death came through the enemy satan).

Ps 146:3-4; "Do not put your trust in princes nor in a son of man, in whom there is no help. His spirit (Heb. = "Ruach" = wind or breath) departs, he returns to his earth; in that day his plans perish."

Eccl 3:19; "For what happens to the sons of men also happens to the beasts; one thing befalls them; <u>as one dies, so dies the other</u>, surely they all have one breath; <u>man has</u> <u>no advantage over the beast</u>, for all is vanity."

Job 7:9-10; "So he who goes down to the grave <u>does not come up</u>. He shall never return to his house.

Eccl 9:5; "For the living know that they will die. But <u>the dead know nothing</u>, and they have no more reward, for the memory of them is forgotten."

Eccl 9:10; "Whatever your hand finds to do, do it with all your might; for <u>there is</u> <u>no work or devise</u> <u>or knowledge or wisdom in the grave</u> where you are going."

Heb 11:13, speaking of the patriarchs of old states; "These all died in the faith, <u>not</u> <u>having</u> <u>received the promises</u>, but having seen them afar off

28

embraced them, and confessed they were strangers and pilgrims on the earth." Verse 39; "And all these, having obtained a good testimony through faith, did not receive the promise."

John 6:49; "your fathers ate the manna in the wilderness and <u>are dead</u>."

1 Tim 6:15-16; "…the King of kings and Lord of lords, <u>Who alone has</u> <u>immortality</u>, dwelling in unapproachable light, whom no man has seen or can see, to whom be honor and everlasting power."

Matt 22:31-32; "But concerning the resurrection of the dead have you not read what was spoken to you by God saying I am the God of Abraham, the God of Isaac, and the God of Jacob? God is not the God of the dead, but of the living."

Today He is our God, as we live, just as He was their God when they were alive. He is a Living God of the living. Satan is a dead god of the dead. If we choose to follow Yehweh we live. If we choose to follow satan we die. Yeshua holds the keys and is the door to the Way. Each has a path to follow and one is broad and one is narrow. One path is easy and one is hard. One says we are immortal, as gods, and surely won't die and one says we are mortal, just like all the animals, and do in fact die. This brings us to face the resurrection.

John 3:13; "<u>No one has ascended to heaven but he who came down from heaven,</u> that is the Son of Man who is in heaven."

John 5:26-29; "For as the Father has life in Himself, so He has granted the Son to have life in Himself, and has given Him authority to execute judgment also, because He is the Son of Man. Do not marvel at this; <u>for the hour is coming in which all who are in</u> <u>the graves</u> will hear His voice and come forth—those who have done good to the resurrection of life (foremost or first resurrection) and those who have done evil to the resurrection of condemnation.

John 6:40; "… and I will raise him up <u>on the last day</u>."

Verse 44; "No one can come to Me unless the Father who sent Me draws him, and <u>I will raise him up on the last day</u>."

Verse 54; "Whoever eats My flesh and drinks My blood has eternal life, <u>and I will</u> <u>raise him up on the last day</u>.

1 Cor 15:20-23; "But Christ is risen from the dead, and has become the first fruits of those who have fallen asleep. For since by man came death, by Man also came the resurrection of the dead. For as in Adam all die, even so in Christ all shall be made alive. <u>But each in his own order</u>: Christ the

first fruits, <u>afterward</u> those who are Christ's <u>at His coming</u>" (not when we die).

1 Thes 4:16; "For the Lord Himself will descend from heaven with a shout, with the voice of an archangel, and with the trumpet of God. <u>And the dead in Christ will rise</u> first. Then we who are alive and remain (also in Christ) shall be caught up together with them in the clouds to meet the Lord in the air."

Those who rise first are those who are part of the first (the first order or rank) resurrection mentioned in Rev 20:5. Verse 6 says; "…over such the second death has no power." Others resurrected will still be subject to that second and everlasting death. They are of the resurrection of condemnation.

At the resurrection Matt 24:31 says; "And He will send His angels with a great sound of trumpet, and they will gather His elect from the four winds." This thought is remembered through the Feast of Trumpets and is also restated in Mark 13:27. And who is His elect? His church, who are the ones called out of this worlds system, which He has drawn to know, embrace, and follow His ways, now in this dark age as a reflective light to Gods glory. John 6:44 "No one can come to Me unless the Father who sent Me <u>draws him</u> (No preacher can do this), and I will raise him up <u>at the last day</u>." Col 3:12 also defines the elect saying; "Therefore <u>as the elect of God</u>, holy and beloved, put on tender mercies, kindness, humility, meekness, longsuffering, bearing with one another, and forgiving one another, if anyone has a complaint against another, even as Christ forgave you, so you also must do." The elect are bound in faith, just as Paul was, and is stated in the opening phrase of Titus 1:1; "Paul, a bond servant of God and an apostle of Jesus Christ, <u>according to the faith of God's elect</u> and the acknowledgement of the truth which accords with godliness."

From all the above given scriptures we can now see that man dies and immortality is a lie of satan. Our immortality lies in a hope, but is assured through the resurrection of the Christ, and our subsequent resurrection at His coming.

The elects judgment is sure however, as 1 Peter 4:17 states; "For the time has come for judgment to begin at the house of God, and if it begins with us what will be the end of those who do not obey the gospel of God?" Also Romans 8:30; "Moreover whom He predestined, these He also called, these He also justified, and whom He justified, these He also glorified." Once again the thought of the assurance of the elect is repeated in Rom 11:7; "What then? Israel (not just Judah) <u>has not obtained</u> what it seeks, <u>but the elect have obtained it</u>, and the rest were blinded." That assurance is predicated on the thought that the unpardonable sin is not committed and that is given in Matt 12:31;"Therefore I say to you, every sin and blasphemy will be forgiven men, but the blasphemy against the Spirit will not be forgiven men."

The hope of immortality is once again given in Titus 3:7;"… that having been justified by His grace we should become heirs according to <u>the hope of eternal life</u>." It's given again in 1 Thes 2:19; "For <u>what is our hope</u>, or joy, or crown of rejoicing? Is it not even in the presence of our Lord Jesus Christ <u>at His coming</u>?" Once again, notice, this is not at our time of death.

There are several scriptures that are used today to give us that immortality in heaven or hell (an old English word which means a hole in the ground) at our death. If that were the case then all the other scriptures quoted here would have to be eliminated to preserve the faultlessness of Yehweh. A dichotomy of scriptural meaning, resulting in confusion, can only come from the author of confusion so we need to look into the original language more carefully.

2 Cor 5:8 is one of those scriptures; "We are confident, (Greek = "Tharrheo" = to be of good cheer or bold, not <u>to be interpreted as assured of</u>) yes well pleased rather to be absent (Greek = "Ekdemeo" = to go abroad, to emigrate, or to live abroad) from the body and to be present (Greek = "Endemeo" = to

dwell in ones own country, to be among ones own people, to stay at home) with the Lord." And when according to the scriptures do we tabernacle with the Lord? At his coming and our resurrection!

Another scripture also used and that stands alone, if so used, is Luke 16:19-31. It is the parable (a short story used to teach some truth, which often times even the disciples did not understand) of the rich man and Lazarus (a Hebrew name meaning God is helper). It would also help to consider the theme of the whole sixteenth chapter which is stewardship with the wealth of God verses money. Christ is addressing the Pharisees, who were lovers of money and not so much of the word of God, and had turned up their noses at Christ's teaching. He derides them, and reminds them that not even the smallest stroke of the Torah will fail, and then speaks of divorce as a reference to marrying another church whose ways are adulterous and corrupt. It then goes on with the parable of the rich man and the beggar. The Pharisees would not even give a crumb to the poor of Judah even though they possessed the riches of the bread of life in the word of Moses and the Prophets and Writings. Even the parable states that Abraham said "they have Moses and the prophets; let them hear them." (Did you hear them as quoted above?) The other thing that should be noted is that Lazarus does not go to the bosom of Christ who is raised, but

Abraham only. This fits John 3:13 where it states "no one has ascended to heaven but He who came down." The word used in verse 23 for "being in torments" is the Greek "Basasos" which means a touch stone, which is black and used to test the purity of gold or silver by the color of the streak produced by rubbing it with the metal. We too are to be refined and tested and so this may well refer to that separation and judgment of God at the resurrection, once again on the last day and not at or death, as so aptly described in the Torah, Prophets, and Writings, and confirmed in the New Testament as referenced in 1 Cor 15:52; "when the dead <u>will be</u> raised incorruptible, and we <u>shall be</u> changed."

Think of it logically. If we die and go to heaven then why is there a resurrection of the dead at Christ's futuristic coming? We would already be raised would we not? If we are separated after death to heaven and hell, then we are already judged so why is there a judgment yet in the future? If we are indeed only passing through to heaven or hell then we are in fact immortal and satan did not lie to Eve but God did. If we have eternal blessing or damnation then why and what is the second death mentioned of in Revelation? The Scriptural answer is that we are mortal, we die, and we await the resurrection and judgment all in its' proper order.

CHAPTER 6

Where Do We Go When Resurrected?

Rev 11:15 states; "...and the kingdoms (i.e. Sovereignty) <u>of this world</u> (Greek = "Kosmos" = orderly arrangement, the world, the universe, the circle of the earth, the inhabitants of the earth) have become the kingdoms of our Lord and of His Christ, and He shall reign forever and ever." Remember the Lord's Prayer? Your Kingdom come, Your will be done <u>on earth</u> as it is in heaven. His kingdom and His will are coming to this earth and it is not here now. It will be as the King arrives.

Rev 5:9-10 says of the Christ; "...and have redeemed us to God by your blood. Out of every tribe and tongue and people and nation, and have made us kings and priests to our God and <u>we shall reign on the earth</u>.

Isaiah 24:23; "…,for the Lord of hosts <u>will reign on Mount Zion and in Jerusalem</u> and before His elders gloriously."

Joel 2:32; "And it shall come to pass that whoever calls on the name of the LORD (Yahweh) shall be saved. For <u>in Mount Zion and in Jerusalem</u> there shall be deliverance, as the LORD has said, among the remnant whom the LORD calls."

Obed 1:17; "But on Mount Zion there shall be deliverance, and there shall be holiness, the house of Jacob (Israel) shall posses their possessions." Verse 20; "and the captives of this host of children of Israel shall possess the land of the Canaanites as far as Zarephath."(A city of the Sidonians, in other words the whole land of Canaan).Verse 21; "Then saviors shall come to Mount Zion to judge the mountains of Esau, and the kingdom shall be the LORD'S."

Micah 4:7; "I will make the lame a remnant and the outcast a strong nation, so the Lord will reign over them <u>in Mount Zion</u> from now on, even forever."

Some try to spiritualize Mount Zion as being in Heaven but in Zech 14:4 it says; "And in that day

His feet will stand <u>on the Mount of Olives</u>, which faces Jerusalem on the east. And the mount will split in two, from the east to the west, making a very large valley, half of the mountain shall move toward the north and half of it towards the south." Verse 8; "And in that day it shall come to be that living waters shall flow <u>from Jerusalem</u>, half of them toward the eastern sea and half of them toward the western sea; both in summer and winter it shall occur." This is all physically here on the earth with its seasons still cycling. Changed and purified for sure, but still right here.

Rev 22:1-2; "And he showed me a pure river of water of life, clear as crystal, proceeding from the throne of God and of the Lamb. In the middle of its street, on either side of the river, was a tree of life, which bore twelve fruits, each yielding its fruit every month. And the leaves were for the healing of the nations."

Ezek 47:1-12 repeats the description of this same river <u>in Jerusalem</u>.

The whole of the second Psalm is the coronation of Christ on the earth and the nations of the earth who rage against Him.

Isaiah 11:9-16; "They shall not hurt nor destroy in all My holy mountain, for <u>the earth</u> shall be full

* *Witness the Truth - Are You Being Deceived* *

of the knowledge of the LORD as the waters cover the sea. And in that day there shall be a root of Jesse, who shall stand as a banner to the people, for the gentiles shall seek Him, and His resting place shall be glorious. It shall come to pass in that day that the LORD shall set His hand again for the second time to recover the remnant (futuristic) of His people who are left, from Assyria and Egypt, from Pathos and Cush, from Elam and Shinar, from Hanath and the islands of the sea. (Again all places here on the earth) He will set up a banner for the nations, and will assemble the outcasts of Israel (not just Judah), and gather together the dispersed of Judah <u>from the corners of the earth</u>. Also the envy of Ephriam shall depart, and the adversaries of Judah shall be cut off, Ephriam shall not envy Judah, and Judah shall not harass Ephriam. But they shall fly down upon the shoulder of the Philistines toward the west; together they shall plunder the people of the East, they shall lay their hand on Edom and Moab; and the people of Ammon shall obey them. The LORD will utterly destroy the tongue of the Sea of Egypt (again on the earth), with His mighty wind He will shake His fist over the river, and strike it in the seven streams, and make men cross over dry-shod. There will be a highway for the remnant of His people who will be left from Assyria, as it was for Israel in that day he came up from the land of Egypt."

39

As we can see all these are references to places here on the earth and not in some spiritual place. Eccl 1:4 even states that; "one generation passes away, and another generation comes, <u>but the earth abides</u> (Heb. = "Omaadet" = to stand, endure, continue) <u>forever</u>." Then what is the meaning of 2Peter 3:10 where it seems to say that the earth will be melted? It reads; "But the day of the Lord will come as a thief, in which the heavens will pass away (Gk. = "Pareleusontai" = to pass near or by) with a great noise, and the elements (Gk. = "Stoicheion" = the rudiments or elements, fundamental principles) will melt with fervent heat; both the earth (Gk. = "Gee" = contracted from a primary word, soil; by extension a region, or the solid part of a whole, the ground, the earth as a standing place, a country, land enclosed within fixed boundaries, the land as opposed to the sea) and the works that are in it will be burned up (Gk. = "Katakakeesetai" = to burn down to the ground, i.e. consume wholly)."

First we must remember that the earth is indeed reserved for fire for 2 Peter 3:7 states; "But the heavens and the earth which are now preserved by the same word <u>are reserved for fire</u> until the day of judgment and perdition (Gk. = "Apoleia" = ruin or loss, destruction) of ungodly men." Notice it speaks of the destruction of the ungodly here and not the earth as such. The elements are the rudiments or rudimental underpinnings of this age of satan, being the strife, envy, pride, jealousy, hatred, bitterness, deceit, and self-seeking. It is such as this that is destroyed with the brightness of His coming. The new earth spoken of in Rev. 21:1 is the Greek word "Kainon" and denotes freshness or refreshing. Remember too that people are resurrected to a spiritual body at His coming, as shown earlier, and so the cleansing of the earth with fire would not destroy them.

A complete study of the use of the word fire, especially as used in the Psalms, would also add light to the subject of the cleansing and destruction at the coming of Yeshua. Remembering too the spiritual/physical aspect of Gods word will also give a more clear big picture. God has given both satan and us time. We are to choose a way of life and he doesn't close any door until He has given His Christ time also. That is what the one thousand year millennial reign is all about. It is also what the second death is all about after all have experienced those ways of life both under satan and the Christ's governing. Our Father is more than fair, but He is also unbending. It's Life and Death and the choice is ours to make. Are your eyes and ears open or closed to His Truth? Satan's way, for now, is always easier and more comfortable. Sort of like being convinced that you're saved, or doing Gods' work, with out ever even knowing God's name, let alone His requirements for your salvation or work. The destination is either a short ride with the father of lies or an endless one with the Yehweh and His Family.

From the above study we should be able to see that the earth remains, though cleansed (Ref also Isaiah 14:7, and Ps 104:30, and 2 Chron 36:21) and Yeshua (Christ) and His elect reign on the earth after being resurrected to establish the Kingdom of God.

CHAPTER 7

The Gathering of the Nations for Teaching and Salvation.

The gentile nations are gathered to Him at His coming and His people are separated from them. Matt 25:32; "All the nations (Gk. = "Ethnos" = a non Jewish or Israelite tribe or people usually pagan) will be gathered before Him, and He will separate one from another, as a shepherd divides his sheep from the goats." Also Ezek 20:38; "I will purge the rebels from among you, and those who transgress against Me; I will bring them out of the country where they sojourn, but they shall not enter the land of Israel."

Psalms 72:11; "Yes all kings shall fall down before Him; All nations shall serve Him."

Of <u>Israel</u> He says in Ezek verse 41 & 42; "I will accept you as a sweet aroma when <u>I bring you out from the peoples and gather you out of the countries where you</u> have been scattered; and I will be hallowed in you before the Gentiles. Then you shall know that I am the Lord, when I bring you into the land of Israel, into the country for which I lifted My hand in an oath to your fathers."

Psalms 97 sums up the whole; "The LORD reigns; let the earth rejoice; let the multitude of the isles be glad! Clouds of darkness surround Him. Righteousness and justice are the foundation of His throne. A fire goes before Him, and burns up His enemies round about. His lightnings light the world; the earth sees and trembles. The mountains (usually depicting governments or kingdoms) melt like wax at the presence of the LORD, at the presence of the Lord of the whole earth. The heavens declare His righteousness, and all the people see His glory..."

Romans 11:17-33 speaking to the gentiles, says of Israel in verse 23 & 24; "And they (Judah and Israel) also, if they do not continue in unbelief, will be grafted in, for God is able to graft them in again. For if you (the gentiles) were cut out of the olive tree which is wild by nature, and were grafted contrary to nature into a cultivated olive tree how much more will these, who are natural branches, be grafted into their own olive tree?"

The 98th Psalms has even more to add. "Oh sing to the LORD a new song! For He has done a marvelous thing, His right hand and His holy arm have gained the victory. <u>The LORD has made known His salvation</u>, His righteousness He has revealed in the sight of the nations. He has remembered His mercy and His faithfulness to the house of Israel (not just Judah, but that whole nation of Israel that is as the sands of the sea) all the ends of the earth have seen the salvation of our God. Shout joyfully to the LORD with harp and the sound of a psalm, with trumpets and the sound of a horn, shout joyfully before the LORD the King. (Isn't it nice to know that God encourages good and glad music?) Let the sea roar, and all its fullness, the world and those who dwell in it. Let the rivers clap their hands; let the hills be joyful together before the LORD, for He is coming to judge the earth. With righteousness He shall judge the world, and the people with equity."

Psalm 84 is all about Israel (not Judah alone) in the tabernacle of God in Zion. Psalms 102, 107, and 110 all support the same theme as does Ps 132:13-18; "For the LORD has chosen Zion, He has desired it for His dwelling place; This is My resting place forever, here I will dwell, for I have desired it. I will abundantly bless her provision; I will satisfy her poor with bread. I will also clothe her priests with salvation, and her saints shall shout for joy. There I will make the horn of David grow; I will prepare a lamp for My Anointed. His enemies I will clothe with shame, but upon Himself His crown shall flourish."

Isaiah 2 shows that not only will the kingdom be established over all nations but that they will flow to it to be taught and corrected. That teaching job is for the priests and kings of God who are the blessed of the first (foremost) resurrection (Rev 5:10). It is also why salvation and judgment will be fair to everyone. All get to know and choose before they are finally judged.

Verse 2-4 of Isaiah 2; "Now it shall come to pass that in the latter days that the mountain of the Lord's house shall be established on the top of the mountains, and shall be exalted above the hills; and all the nations shall flow to it. Many people shall come and say, Come, and let us go up to the mountain of the LORD, to the house of the God of Jacob (Israel); He will teach us His ways, (salvation is still available) and we shall walk in His paths. For out of Zion shall go forth the law (Heb. = "Torah" = law, obviously not done away with but the same yesterday, today, and always), and the word of the LORD from Jerusalem. He shall judge between the nations, and rebuke many people (remember that broad wide path to destruction is full of so called Christians and non Christians alike), they shall beat their swords into plowshares, and their spears into pruning hooks; nation shall not lift up the sword against nation, neither shall they learn war anymore."

Isaiah 30 speaks of this millennial time too, and verse 20 -21 speaks of the teaching that will be ongoing when it says; "… yet your <u>teachers</u> will not be moved into a corner anymore, but your eyes shall see your teachers. Your ears shall hear a word behind you saying, this is the way, walk in it, whenever you turn to the right hand or whenever you turn to the left" (Salvation through Truth).

Isaiah 65:20; "No more shall an infant from there (Jerusalem) live but a few days, nor an old man who has not fulfilled his days, for the child shall die one hundred years old, but the sinner being one hundred years shall be accursed." These resurrected people are given their first chance to know the LORD while not under satan's deceptive sway, as he is bound for the thousand year reign (Rev 20:2). They will be tested however, as satan is released for a little while (Rev 20:3). Salvation is there as well as the second death and is made final at the Great White throne Judgment as depicted by the last great day of the Feast of Tabernacles, which is also a depiction of when we live or tabernacle with God.

Zech 8:3-8 continues to witness the same pattern of thought; "Thus says the LORD, I will return to Zion and dwell in the midst of Jerusalem. Jerusalem shall be called the City of Truth, the Mountain of the LORD of hosts, the Holy Mountain…Old men and old women shall again sit in the streets of Jerusalem, each one with his staff in his hand because of great age. The streets of the city shall be full of boys and girls playing in its streets…. Behold <u>I will save</u> My people from the land of the east and from the land of the west (salvation) I will bring them back, and they shall dwell in the midst of Jerusalem. They shall be My people and I will be their God, in truth and righteousness." Verse 13; "and it shall come to pass that just as you were a curse among the nations, O <u>house of Judah</u> <u>and house of Israel</u>, so <u>I will save you</u>.(again salvation) and you shall be a blessing."

Isaiah 4:1-6; "In that day seven women shall take hold of one man (one of the priests and kings of the LORD) saying, we will eat our own food and wear our own apparel, only let us be called by your name, to take away our reproach. (Here the ethnic diversity remains but salvation is given as they choose to take on the Way of God) In that day the Branch of the LORD shall be beautiful and glorious, and the fruit of the earth shall be excellent and appealing for those of Israel (not just Judah) who have escaped. And it shall come to pass that he who is left in Zion and the remnant in Jerusalem will be called   holy—everyone who is recorded among the living in Jerusalem. When the LORD has washed away the filth of the daughters of Zion, and purged the blood of Jerusalem from her midst, by the spirit of judgment and by the spirit of burning, then the LORD will create above every dwelling place of Mount Zion, and above her assemblies, a cloud and smoke by day and the shining of a flaming fire by night. For over all the glory there will be a covering. And there will be a tabernacle for shade in the daytime from the heat, for a place of refuge, and for a shelter from the storm and rain (This is again on the earth and in the future).

Zech 2:11; "Many nations shall be joined to the LORD in that day, and they shall become My people (again salvation is still available) and I will dwell in your midst (again on the earth).Then you will know that the LORD of hosts has sent Me to you."

Zech 14:16 – 17; "And it shall come to pass that everyone who is left of all the nations which came up against Jerusalem shall go up from year to year (this is during the one thousand year reign or the millennium) to worship the King, the LORD of hosts, and to keep the Feast of Tabernacles. And it shall be that whichever of the families of the earth do not come up to Jerusalem to worship the

King, the LORD of hosts, on them there will be no rain."

If you are a follower of "Christ", do you even know what the Feast of Tabernacles is or when it was instituted and by whom? If you are not a follower of "Christ" it obviously still applies to the worship of Yehweh. Or don't you believe what is written in Scripture? Anything less is from the god of this world (Satan, 2Cor 4:4)!

Isaiah 11:4 – 9 speaking of the Christ at that time of millennial rest says; "But with righteousness He shall judge the poor, and decide with equity for the meek of the earth, He shall strike the earth with the rod of His mouth, and with the breath of His lips He shall slay the wicked. Righteousness shall be the belt of His loins, and faithfulness the belt of His waist. The wolf also will dwell with the lamb, the leopard shall lie down with the young goat, the calf and the young lion and the fatling together, and a little child shall lead them. The cow and the bear shall graze; their young shall lie down together and the lion shall eat straw like the ox. The nursing child shall play by the cobra's hole, and the weaned child shall put his hand in the vipers den. They shall not hurt nor destroy in all My holy mountains for the earth shall be full of the knowledge of the LORD as the waters cover the sea."

Isaiah 65:25 witnesses to the same thought of Isaiah 11. "The wolf and the lamb shall feed together, the lion shall eat straw like the ox, and dust shall be the serpents' food. They shall not hurt nor destroy in all My holy mountain, says the LORD." Oh to be gathered to the LORD in Truth!

CHAPTER 8

Who are the Gentiles and Who is Israel?

The gentiles are the "Aadam" children and Israel is the "Et Ha Aadam" children with satan's children scattered among them all as tares. To be sure that is an overly simplistic statement and over the millennium the blending has made it all but impossible to identify them both, as such, with any accuracy.

The grafting in through Yeshua and the spiritual salvation open to all, including the tares, makes it all a mute point anyway except that God put a greater responsibility on the Israeli people as we see from Luke 12:47-48; "And that servant, who knew his masters will, and did not prepare himself or do according to his will, shall be beaten with many stripes. But he who did not know, yet committed things deserving stripes, shall be beaten with few. <u>For everyone to whom much is given, from him much will be required,</u> <u>and to whom much has been committed, of him they will ask the more</u>."

Look to the leading Christian nations and peoples and ask yourself honestly, many stripes or few? Now narrow it down to yourself.

Israel was originally the twelve sons of Jacob, who was renamed Israel after he wrestled with God (Gen 32:28). They stayed a nation of twelve tribes, headed by the brothers, until Israel blessed Josephs' two sons Manasseh and Ephraim, when in Egypt (Gen 48:16), and said "let my name be named upon them." That actually made thirteen tribes but since the tribe of Levi was the priestly tribe, and so was given a tithe of all and not an actual inheritance, they were still considered as twelve. After King Solomon died they split between the tribes of Judah, Benjamin, and Levi, which became known and referred to as the southern tribe of Judah, and the remaining ten tribes of the north, which were then known and referred to as Israel (1Kings 12:16-33). There was then war between Israel and Judah all the days of their kings (1Kings 14:30 and 15:16).

Historically, the Northern Tribe of Israel corrupted themselves first and were subsequently defeated and taken captive by the Assyrians and removed from the land "as it is to this day" (2 Kings 17:23) in 721-718 b.c.e.. They became known as the "Diaspora" or the lost ten tribes. In Deut 32:26 God says of them; "I will dash them to pieces, I will make the memory of them to cease from among men." This is not talking of Judah, who was never lost and never forgotten, but Israel (the lost ten tribes), who is lost among men but never from God.

Judah then corrupted herself, as well, and was defeated and taken captive by Babylon (2 Kings 24:14) in 597 b.c.e. Judah then returned to Jerusalem to rebuild, fulfilling the seven hundred year old prophesy of Cyrus (2Chron 36:22). The Jews remain but Israel is gone and <u>the two cannot be interchanged</u>. Confusion exists today because the Jews from around the world were given the land of Israel again in 1948. They are still Judah only. Ask any one from there, and he will tell you, he is a Jew from here, or there, but always a Jew. Believe them, they know who they are. Do they ever claim to be from Zebulun, or Issachar, Naphtali, or Gad? Can you even name the rest? Can they?

There are several books that deal with the lost tribes. The afore mentioned <u>Tracing our Ancestors</u> and <u>The United States and Britain in Prophecy</u> by H. Armstrong. They both deal with the identity and blessing of Israel but neglect the curse that goes with the dispersion (Deut 28), due to a rejection of the one true God and His ways, that was given unto them through His Torah. It continues throughout the so called "Christianity" of Israel (not just Judah) today but is no better than the tripe given under Jeroboam, the appointed King of Israel after Solomon died, that got them into trouble so long ago. There surely is "Nothing new under the sun" is there?

CHAPTER 9

Babylonian Mystery Religion

Babylonian Mystery Religion is the great harlot described in Rev. 17:1; "...Come, I will show you the judgment of the great harlot who sits on many waters, with whom the kings of the earth committed fornication, and the inhabitants of the earth were made drunk with the wine of her fornication." She is a false religion that does not follow the Biblical ways of God as outlined in the Bible and she is described as being the mother of harlots that come out of her and do the same. She is also described as being "drunk with the blood of the martyrs of Jesus".

Ask yourself what great religion has killed the saints, been in power over the kings of the earth, and had other harlots come out of her? Don't forget that the churches that come out of her are just as corrupt.

We assure you that they all will be worshiping God as "Christians" but not Biblically. They will all claim to be the true way and have the correct path, and power, but Babylon is confusion and when viewed as a whole the confusion is evident. Do you suppose they even agree among themselves? Does "broad wide path to destruction" start to scare you? The thundering of God should! Add in all the churches that don't follow Yeshua at all and it really becomes chaotic.

Isaiah 1:13-18; "Bring no more futile sacrifices, and the calling of assemblies—I cannot endure iniquity and the sacred meeting. <u>Your</u> New Moons and <u>your</u> appointed feasts <u>My soul hates</u>. (This is GOD talking to us here) They are a trouble to Me, I am weary of bearing them. When you spread your hands, <u>I will hide</u> My eyes from you; Even though you make many prayers, <u>I will not hear</u>, your hands are full of blood. Wash yourself, make yourself clean; Put away the evil of your doings from before My eyes. Cease to do evil, learn to do good; Seek Justice, Reprove the oppressor, Defend the fatherless, Plead for the widow. Come now, and let us reason together says the Lord. Though your sins are like scarlet, they shall be white as snow, though they are red like crimson, they shall be as wool; If you are <u>willing and obedient</u>, You shall eat the good of the land, but if you refuse and rebel, you shall be devoured by the sword, for the mouth of the Lord has spoken it."

If that doesn't hit home there is more; Amos 5:21; "I hate, I despise your feast days, and I do not savor your sacred assemblies." Does that sound like our churches are in favor with the Father to you? Again in Mal 2:3 God thunders; "Behold I will rebuke your descendants and spread refuse on your faces, the refuse of your solemn feasts, and one will take you away with it." The word used for refuse or dung in the King James is the Hebrew word "Peresh". It translates excrement, offal, or fecal matter. A more disgusting word could not be used and still be from God.

If you still think it doesn't apply to you or your worship read Isaiah 29:13; "In as much as these people draw near to Me with their mouths , and honor Me with their lips, but have removed their hearts far from Me, and their fear toward Me is taught by the commandments of men." It continues through the end of the chapter to describe the millennial reign where the deaf will hear and the blind will see and the poor among men will rejoice in the Holy One of Israel (not Judah) and when the terrible one is brought to nothing. Did you ever read what Yeshua said of lip service? Matt 15:8; "These people draw near to Me with their mouth, and honor Me with their lips, but their heart is far from Me. <u>And in vain they worship Me</u>, teaching as doctrine the commandments of men." He repeats the same for emphasis in Mark 7:6. The scary thing is He is talking about "Christians" as if the rest of the religions are not bad enough.

He adds further insult to injury in Matt 7:22-23 by saying; "Many will say to Me in that day, Lord, Lord, have we not prophesied in Your name, cast out demons in your name, and done many wonders in your name? And I then will declare to them, I never knew you, <u>depart from Me, you who practice lawlessness</u>!" Can you imagine being a member of a Christian church doing many wonders in Christ's' name and being told "I never knew you"? There obviously has to be something drastically wrong with the doctrines of so called worship and assembly in our churches. And that something according to Christ has to do with lawlessness.

If you look at the major festivals of modern Christianity you will find the universal ones to be Easter, Christmas, Halloween, Valentines Day, Mardi Grau, Lent, and Epiphany or Ash Wednesday. Then there is the May pole, the rolling of eggs, Easter bunnies, sun rise services, Mary worship, prayers to saints, and repetitive prayers, holy water, speaking in tongues with no interpretation, indulgences, intercessions, confessions, knock down healings, and exorcisms of all kinds of maladies, rapture of the saints, the trinity doctrine that refutes the one true God, and the sinners prayer of acceptance, just to name a few off the top of the head.

There is one God, Yehweh, and He has written us a love letter that we call the Holy Bible, to direct us on the path to Him. He has redeemed us to Him through His Son Yeshua if we choose to follow. We can look to the past historically, or the future prophetically, and we will always see the unchangeable God but He is always distorted in the present by the god of this world.

We could go to our brother Judah to learn a lot and vise versa. Grace and Law are from the same source and compliment each other. Sorry to say, but habitual pride really comes into its own here on both sides.

"Christians" will right away say what is wrong with Christmas and Easter? Certainly they are celebrated in His name, but are they of God or man? Let's start with Christmas. In the first place Yeshuah's birth can be calculated from John the Baptist who was six months older (Luke 1:26). John's birth can be calculated by his father Zacharias's course of service, which was the division of Abijah, (Luke 1:5) the eighth, (1Chron 24:10) being in June or July depending on the moon. Nine months later

John would have been born in March or April. That made Yeshua's birth in September or October.

There are other sources that pin point Christ's birth on the first day of the Feast of Tabernacles in the year 4 b.c.e., but there is no certainty for that kind of accuracy, other than good common sense. He did indeed come to tabernacle among men and for certain it was in the fall at the time of the feasts. Even to this day the flocks are not kept in the fields around Jerusalem past November due to the rains and cold (Luke 2:8). Secondly; The Bible states in Eccl 7:1; "A good name is better than precious ointment, and the day of ones' death than the day of ones' birth." If God says Passover, the day we know to be the day our Lord died, is better than the day of our Lord's birth, which we are unsure of but certainly is not in December, then wouldn't you think it wise to celebrate the one He gave us and not the other?

A passing glance study of Christmas will show it to be saturated in paganism, with the world deceived into honoring it. The fruit of the season is over spending, theft, drunkenness, family fights, loneliness, and selfishness in gifting with the day after Christmas being the second biggest business day as all the gifts are exchanged or returned. The billboards tell us to keep Christ in Christmas but, the fact is, He was never there in the first place.

Ishtar (Pronounced "Easter") was the mistress of the sun god (His day was celebrated on Dec 25th), and the goddess of sex and fertility. Our present Easter celebration with rabbits, sunrise services, May poles, and eggs are old fertility rights. The real question is when did Christ die? This became lost beginning with the schism of Polycrates and Polycarp, the bishops of the first century eastern and western churches. It is what separated the early Jerusalem church from Rome in the first century. Sabbath and Passover were considered "Judaizing" and what came out of the dark ages was the final council of Nicene in 325 c.e. where all of the first century church teachings were substituted with the refuse we follow now.

The reason the day is important is that the Bible states that the only sign that would be given that Yeshua was in fact the messiah was that He would be three days and three nights in the grave (Luke 11:29).If He died on Good Friday and was raised on Easter Sunday then He was only in the grave one day and two nights (thirty-six hours) and so, by His own mouth, He is not the messiah. To say the Jew counted different is tripe. The Jewish Yeshua asks us in John 11:9; "Are there not twelve hours in a day?" That leaves twelve hours in what is called a night as the earth has always turned in twenty-four hours. Three days and three nights are, and were, seventy-two hours! Either Easter is a lie, or deception, or Yeshua Himself is.

We need to look at the annual Sabbath of the First Day of Unleavened Bread, instead of the weekly Sabbath, when we consider the preparation day that He was taken down from the stake. Passover in 31 c.e. fell on a Wednesday and so Thursday was a High Sabbath (the first day of unleavened bread). If He died, as Gods sacrificial lamb, on Wednesday evening (Passover) then He would have been in the grave the scriptural three days and three nights and risen on Saturday. They then went to the grave after the weekly Sabbath and found the grave empty. That would have been on the Sunday within the Feast of Unleavened Bread, when He ascended as the acceptable offering before the LORD, at the exact same time that the high priest waved the Sheaf Wave Offering of the first fruits of the barley harvest.

Yeshua was in fact our first fruit of all those to be resurrected in the future. He is also our Passover, but satan has deceived us into believing another lie to confuse the issue and leave doubt in the minds of those who question his Babylonian churches. Thankfully, by going to the Bible in its original language and historical facts, we can still expose the lies. Whether we are too comfortable to take the narrow road is yet another question. There are other works that document this truth as well, with the <u>Companion Bibles appendix #164 & 165</u> being one of them.

Now, since once again the Bible is our standard for Truth, look and see how many of those mainstream church holidays are recorded and taught by God as His commandment or covenant. None! Now go to Lev 23:1; "And the LORD (Our Father Yehweh) spoke to Moses, saying speak to the children of Israel (not Judah alone) and say to them, the feasts of the LORD, which you shall proclaim to be holy convocations, these are My (Gods' given to us to honor Him) feasts." Ouch! Now do you see why it would be advantageous to recognize who Israel really is? This is to them and much is expected of them. Israel was to teach his children and the gentile as well, His Truth through them. Since the only truth in mans days of tradition might be a sincere effort in a losing game, wouldn't it be nice to repent and turn to the Father as he has it written?

He goes on in verse three. "Six days shall work be done, but the seventh is a Sabbath (repose or intermission) of solemn (serious, done with form and ceremony, sacred) rest, a holy convocation (assembly). You shall do no work on it; it is the Sabbath of the LORD in all your dwellings." This is the rest of the Father, again given to us, and is indisputably our Saturday. The day was lost by Israel before and reestablished, during the days of Manna, during Israel's' wandering in the wilderness. That seven day cycle has not been broken or lost since then.

Sunday is the day most modern day churches keep but it is the first day and not the seventh. Most know this already but declare that Yeshua was raised on it. That, as we have shown, is a lie. He was accepted as the sheaf wave offering on a Sunday, as shown, and that day is also to be kept during the Days of Unleavened Bread. Any careful study will show that the first century church kept the same days as did our Lord Yeshua. It broke down during the controversy of Polycarp, who was eventually burned at the stake by the "church" for his Judaizing.

There is one reference to the breaking of bread on the first day in Act 20:7 and that is just what it means. They came together for a common meal. If they kept the Passover meal it was always on Passover, another day of Gods. Dig in your heals if you must, but your kicking against Gods word not ours. 1 Sam 2:29; "Why do you kick at <u>My</u> sacrifice and <u>My</u> offering <u>which I have commanded</u> in <u>My dwelling place</u>, and honor <u>your sons more than Me</u>, to make yourselves fat with the best of all the offerings of Israel My people.

Yeshua is said to be the Lord of the Sabbath in Mark 2:28 and Luke 6:5. He is also "the same yesterday, today, and forever" (Heb 13:8), "an unchangeable priesthood" (Heb. 7:24), "The Alpha and the Omega, the beginning and the end, the first and the last" (Rev. 22:13). Do you think that He came as the Lion of Judah, a Torah observant Jew, just to undo everything that He originated? In Leviticus He says that the Fathers Feasts are to be kept <u>throughout your generations</u> three different times. Does that sound like He wanted them changed? Do a historical study of the ones who have changed them in the past and then ask yourself if they need to be changed again.

Lev 23:4; "These are the feasts of the Lord, holy convocations which you shall proclaim <u>at their appointed times</u>." They are appointed by GOD!

1: (Passover and the Feast of Unleavened Bread) Lev 23:5; "On the fourteenth day of the first month (the new moon after the spring equinox) at twilight is the LORD's Passover. (Notice it is not taken or celebrated weekly or daily)And on the fifteenth day of the same month is the Feast of Unleavened Bread to the LORD, seven days you must eat unleavened bread. On the first day you shall have a holy convocation, you shall do no customary work on it." Verse 8; "...the seventh day (of the weeklong feast of unleavened bread) shall be a holy convocation, you shall do no customary work on it."

2: (Firstfruits) Lev 23:11; "He (the high priest) shall wave the sheaf (of the first fruits of the harvest) before the LORD to be accepted on your behalf; on the day after the Sabbath (within the feast of unleavened bread) the priest shall wave it. Notice no convocation here, just the wave and Yeshua has become that offering.

3: (Pentecost) Lev 23:15; "And you shall count for yourselves from the day after the Sabbath, from the day that you brought the sheaf of the wave offering seven Sabbaths shall be counted. Count fifty days to the day after the seven Sabbaths." Verse 21; "You shall proclaim on the same day that it is a holy convocation to you." Here is where GOD says to keep a Sunday, but not every one, just this once a year occurrence.

4: (Trumpets) Lev 23:24; "In the seventh month on the first day of the month (New moon of Sept or Oct depending on the year) you shall have a Sabbath rest, a memorial of blowing of trumpets, a holy convocation."

5: (Day of Atonement) Lev 23:27; "Also on the tenth day of the seventh month shall be a Day of Atonement. It shall be a holy convocation for you; you shall afflict your souls (fast) and offer an offering made by fire to the Lord. And you shall do no work on that same day, for it is the Day of Atonement, to make atonement for you before the Lord your God."

6: (Tabernacles) Lev 23:34; "…The fifteenth day of this seventh month (full moon) shall be the Feast of Tabernacles for seven days to the Lord. On the first day there shall be a holy convocation. You shall do no work on it." Verse 36; "On the eighth day you shall have a holy convocation." Verse 37; "These are the feasts of the Lord which you shall proclaim to be holy convocations." Verse 41; "…it shall be a statue forever in your generations."

Do you believe the lie that they are done away with as they are an old testament? They are part of the first Covenant. Some are already fulfilled in Yeshua, and some are not, but they will be because they are still very much on the agenda of God. Do your eyes see why they are not on satan's agenda or has he blinded you to their ultimate truth? Satan looses and God wins. Whose side do you want to be on? Satan's lies look good and are easily kept, as long as he is in power, but it won't last forever but Gods will.

Zech 14:16 says of the gentile nations in the millennial reign of Christ that "it shall come to pass that everyone who is left of the gentile nations which came up against Jerusalem shall go up from year to year (this is as the earth still spins around the sun not in some heaven somewhere else) to worship the King, the Lord of hosts <u>and to keep the Feast of Tabernacles</u>. And it shall be that whichever of the families of the earth (again not a heavenly Jerusalem) do not come up to Jerusalem to worship the King, the Lord of hosts, on them there will be no rain. If the family of Egypt will not come up and enter in, they shall have no rain; they shall receive the plague with which the Lord strikes the nations who do not come up to keep the Feast of Tabernacles. This is the punishment of Egypt and the punishment of all the nations that do not come to keep the Feast of Tabernacles."

Do you see Christmas or Halloween, Christianities two biggest days, mentioned here? Egypt celebrates Ramadan was that mentioned either or Africa's Kwanzaa? How about Sunday? We are talking GOD here, and He sets the rules so maybe we ought to pay attention. Even with Christ's second presence some will not obey, how much more now with Him gone? If we are mad or disappointed then it ought to be directed at satan and bring us to repentance, a turning back to God the Father, through the door of His Son our savior. If we do repent, satan is sure to attack us. If we don't, he already has us where he wants us, in his pocket keeping his ways through our traditions and ready to honor him when he shows up before the Christ, acting as the Christ. If you never heard of that, it's little wonder and you need to read on.

CHAPTER 10

The Flood of Lies

In Amos 8:11 God states; "Behold, the days are coming, says the Lord God, that I will send a famine on the land, not a famine of bread, nor of thirst for water, but of the hearing the words of the Lord. They shall wander from sea to sea, from north to east, they shall run to and fro, seeking the word of the Lord, but shall not find it."

What that leaves us with are the lies and deceptions of satan, and if you have read this far, you should be able to see that we are already pretty well steeped in them and here is why. Rev12:13; "Now when the dragon saw that he had been cast to the earth, he persecuted the woman who gave birth to the male child." With a woman being symbolic of a church you need to ask who that was. Christ came out of the tribe of Judah and they have been persecuted indeed, for a long, long time. Verse 17; "And the dragon was enraged with the woman, and he went to make war with the rest of her offspring, who keep the commandments of God and have the testimony of Jesus Christ." The early Judeo-Christian church, which came out of Judah, was also persecuted ferociously because they did indeed keep the commandments of God and have the testimony of Christ. The Jew is still persecuted, even though they deny the Christ, but the Christian church, no longer keeping the commandments, hardly at all.

Look up a word study on persecute, and hate. (Matt 5:11, Matt5:44, Matt 23:34, Luke 11:49, Luke 21:12, John 15:20, and Rom 12:14) It is summed up in John 15:20; "Remember the word that I said to you, a servant is not greater than his master. If they persecuted Me, they will also persecute you. If they kept My word they will keep yours also." Are you and your church persecuted and hated? Do you keep the commandments of God, or even know them, or are you comfortable in a changed set of mans rules? Does your testimony of the Christ even use His name let alone His truth? Are you calling yourself saved and trying to save others and yet ignorant of the Word of God let alone the wiles of satan? Have you said a sinners prayer yet never been buried with Christ in baptism? Have you been baptized but never turned to God and his word? (Repentance) Have you had hands laid upon you? (A fundamental principal of the church of Christ as pointed out in Heb 6:2) Do you call for the elders of the church? Do you even know who they are? Do you know the meaning of the Greek word translated "Church"? It is "Ekklesia" and means the called out ones. They <u>are</u> the church they don't go to one. Or do you just play at "church" telling yourself and others that god has blessed you. If you're at ease in this world then it is satan who has blessed your rebellion of God. Does the mention of the Fathers Holy Days come as a surprise to you or have you already bought into the lie that anything in the Old Covenant is just for "Jews"?

Have you read in Rev 18:4 where God thunders "Come out of her, My people, lest you share in her sins, and lest you receive of her plagues". God is talking about the confusion of Babylon here. If you are to resist her and her confusion do you wear the whole armor of God or even know of what it is comprised of? Do you understand what it is even for? It is to resist the fiery darts or lies of satan (Eph 6:16). There are quite a few "saved" Christians who are facing off with the powers of satan with nothing more than a hat on their head (salvation). Sadly it is only a hat of man's own making and not the armored helmet that God gives through His Word and Spirit. It's our obedience to Him through our spirit that gives us that helmet of protection, let alone the rest of the total armor that we are to be clothed in.

He tells us in Eph. 6:10-13; "Put on the <u>whole armor of God</u>, (Not one of our own making) that you may be able to stand against the wiles (Gk. = "Methodeia" = to lie in wait with trickery) of the devil. For we do not wrestle against flesh and blood, but against principalities (Gk. = "Arche" = a commencement or chief of order, time, place, or rank. The Greek word "Archegos" is a chief leader, or captain, or prince so the meaning is more of <u>time and order</u> as in "that evil day" spoken of in Eph. 6:13 than the person of satan), against powers, against the rulers of the darkness of this age (Here is the person of satan), against spiritual hosts of wickedness in the heavenly places. Therefore take up the whole armor of God, that you might be able to withstand <u>in the evil day</u> (Here is the time element of order), having done all, to stand." Notice it says "Stand" not be taken away as so many would have it today. Eph. 6:14-17 goes on; "Stand therefore, having girded your waist with <u>truth</u>, having put on the breastplate of <u>righteousness</u> (Gk.= ""Dikaiosune"= equity or fairness specifically justification, a freeing from the guilt of sin), and having shod your feet with the <u>preparation of the gospel</u> of peace; above all, taking your shield of <u>faith</u> (Gk.= "Pistis"=persuasion, credence, conviction of truth or the truthfulness of God) with which you will be able to quench all the fiery darts of the wicked one. And take up the helmet of <u>salvation</u>, and the sword of the Spirit, which is the <u>word of God</u>."(Rightly divided or made straight as per 2 Tim 2:15) You see we need to do it all His way and not ours. Is it any wonder the church is in trouble today?

Are you putting on a show but neglecting the essence. There are lots of big mega-show churches that are very popular today. Are you comfortable in one of them? If satan isn't after you, or your church, then it's a pretty good chance that he already has you steeped in his deceptive lies and delusions. Such as are you saved and waiting to be raptured away while the sinful world suffers, rather than standing firm in the truth as we are clothed in the armor spoken of in the above paragraph? The rapture is not in the Bible and the thought is taken out of context. It goes over well because it's comforting. <u>The subject of Matt 24:38 is the flood</u>. In Noah's day it was water, in the end it is a flood of lies and deceptions from the mouth of satan and his "wolves in sheep's clothing" that host our churches pulpits. Verse 38; "For as in the days before the flood, they were eating and drinking, marrying and giving in marriage, until the day that Noah entered the ark, and did not know <u>until the flood</u> came and took them away, <u>so also will the coming of the Son of Man be</u>. Then two men will be in the field one will be taken (by the flood) and the other left."

Christians should want to be left behind working in the field of God and wearing the full armor of God so that when the Master comes He will say "well done you good and faithful servant". Those few left in the field are epitomized by the two witnesses, who stand against satan and his world view (Rev 11:3-12). They expose the coming antichrist and are not taken away by the flood of lies from his mouth because they are well grounded in what is actually written. Are you well grounded? Our hope is that this information will help you to be so inclined. What do you want, the easy way, or the hard, the broad, or the narrow way? When Yeshua said in Luke 12:43; "Blessed is that servant whom the master will find so doing when He comes", He was talking about the one left in the field.

CHAPTER 11

The Appearance of Satan

As seen earlier satan was cast down and he went to "persecute the woman who gave birth to the man child and the offspring that keeps the commandments of God (remember too John 14:15; "If you love Me keep My commandments." Not change or ignore them) and have the testimony of Christ." Why would he do that? Because he cannot stand in the Truth written in the "Tanakh" (Old Testament) which are the "Torah" (Law), the "Nevi'im (Prophets), and the "Kethuvim" (writings), which are preserved to this day by that "woman" or "church" the tribe of Judah. And why does he persecute <u>the</u> <u>commandment keeping</u> New Testament offspring? His persecution is for the same reason as the first. A proper reading of the New Testament condemns him with its truth too. The outcome of that satanic persecution has been that he has been successful enough in his ways that today the Jew denies the Christ and the New Testament church denies, or changes, the law.

Again in 1John 5:19; "...and the whole world lies under the sway of the wicked one". He needs to battle the truth and he does it through the worldwide Babylonian system that embodies his deceptions and half truths as their own truth. That system is set for satan's purpose of self worship and not the worship of Yahweh. The Christ that Babylonian system says they follow is, in fact, the father of lies, the antichrist, or the devil himself. That is why Yeshua will be able to say "I never knew you" and asks if He will "find any faith".

Here we should look up the Greek word for "antichrist". It is a compound word with "Anti" meaning opposite, i.e. instead of, in contrast to, or substitution, and "Christos" meaning anointed, i.e. the messiah. In English when we hear anti, we think of opposite or one who opposes. In the Greek the thought is of <u>an instead of, or substitute,</u> Christ.

2 Thes 2:3; "Let no one deceive you by any means, for that Day (the day of Christ or His second coming) will not come unless the falling away (Greek = "Apostasia" = defection from the truth) comes first, and the man of sin is revealed (Greek =

"Apokalupto" = to take off the cover, to disclose), the son of perdition (Greek = "Apolela" = destruction, ruin, die), who opposes and exalts himself above all that is called God <u>showing himself that he is God</u>". This is also what Matt 24:15 and Mark 13:14 is referencing back to in the book of Daniel and once again shows the seamless continuity of the two covenants.

Here is the purpose and pride of satan in all his power and beauty. He wants to be in the place of God and he has been given a lot of time to accomplish it. We are given the time under him, and then under Yeshua and Yehweh, to choose which God and way of life we intend to follow and be impregnated with.

The defection from Gods Truth and Way should already be evident to you, just from what we have disclosed here in these pages, and the son of perdition will be revealed for what he is as he precedes the True Messiah's coming. We need to be able to distinguish the two different paths and so make our choice wisely.

The first horseman of Revelation is a symbol of that false messiah and what follows him is what always follows him, war, death, famine (of the word), destruction, and petulance. That sequence is also part and parcel with Matt 24, Mark 13, and Luke 21.

There they in their time, and we in ours, are warned of those <u>many</u> that would come <u>in</u> <u>Christ's name</u> deceiving many more. This is why Christ will say "Nevertheless, when the Son of Man comes, will He really find faith on the earth?"(Luke 18:8).

Rev. 9:4 states; "They (The locusts from the bottomless pit) were commanded not to harm the grass of the earth, or any green thing, or any tree, but only those men who do not have the seal (Gk. = "sphragis"= a signet as fencing in or protecting from misappropriation) of God on their foreheads." Will you have the seal of God in your forehead or will you have the mark or the name of the beast? (Rev.13:16) Who are you being led to? Yeshua the Christ with the seal of God or satan the beast as anti-Christ with a phony hat of mans salvation on? Remember He does not say anywhere "just to come as you are" but He repeatedly says to repent! That's a one hundred and eighty degree turn from satan's way to God's. Does the broad path to destruction come to mind? It was true for the first century time, and it is now, and will be yet again as "nothing is new under the sun".

When satan tempted Yeshua he would have given the whole world and its glory if only Yeshua would worship him (Luke 4:5-7). First it should be noted that it was in fact his to give. He really is "the ruler of this world" (John 12:31), "the prince of the power of the air" (Eph 2:2), and "the deceiver of the nations" (Rev 12:9), and what he wants goes all the way back to his fall where "iniquity was found in him" and he thought he could "ascend into heaven and exalt his throne above the stars of God and sit on the mount of the congregation" (Ezek 28:12). He wants to be like the Most High (Isaiah 14:12-15). He wants to be worshiped and he has a church of confusion (Babylonian Mystery Religion) set up to do just that. We are warned in Matt 24:21-22 that it will get so distorted that unless God were to intervene by shortening the time no flesh would be saved. Do you think you are saved? Are your doctrines in line with the two Covenants?

Are you centered on the one true God as introduced in His Word in Deut 6:4-5; "Hear O Israel: (Not just Judah) The Lord (Heb. = Yehweh) our God, the Lord is one! You shall love the Lord your God with all your heart, with all your soul, and with all your might." Or is there another god creeping in to your life? Remember He also states in John 14:15; "If you love Me keep My commandments". His first commandment as given in Exodus 20: 3-4 is; "I am the Lord your God, who brought you out of Egypt, out of the house of bondage. You shall have no other gods before Me. You shall not make for yourselves any carved image, or any likeness of anything that is in heaven above, or that is in the earth beneath, or that is in the water under the earth; you shall not bow down to them nor serve them. For I the Lord your God, am a jealous God, visiting the iniquity of the fathers on the children to the third and fourth generations of those who hate Me, but showing mercy to thousands, to those who love Me and keep My commandments."

And just how do those other gods creep in? Just walk into any religious organizations quarters and what images are there? Are they images given by God or are they graven or carved by the imagination of man? They will vary from the golden statues of gods to the prayer wheels of men. They will depict everything from the people who followed the Christ to the Christ himself and yet even that Christ is only the way or path to the father and not meant to be the object of worship himself. John 14:6; "I am the way, the truth, and the life. No one comes to the Father except through Me." We can't even express enough love to get past the first commandment without putting other gods before our creative Father. We will all claim that those images honor, or depict, God and their beauty is but a reflection of our love. But that's not really what He asks of us is it? We then carry the process one step further by creating the image in our very minds and then arguing over its validity till we have a forced acceptance.

The trinity doctrine may be described as a mystery but as listed in 1 John 5:7 it actually reads; "for there are three that bear record the spirit and the water and the blood and these three in one agree".

The rendering with the words; "in heaven; the Father, the Word, and the Holy Spirit, and these three are one. And there are three that bear witness on earth" is false and misleading. The words that are in italics were all added in the fourth century and are not found in any of the original works. We have already shown where Yeshua is separate from the Father Yehweh and nowhere in the Bible do the apostles greet the Holy Spirit as a person. In fact when it is translated as "he" the original will invariably say "it". It is the power or "Dynamo" of God and not a person.

The Bible clearly states in 1 Cor 8:6; "Yet for us there is one God, the Father, of whom are all things, and we for Him; and one Lord Jesus Christ, through whom all things and through whom we live". The Old Testament is just as clear in Deut. 6:4; "Hear, O Israel: The Lord (Yehweh) our God, the Lord (Yehweh) is one! (Not three) We are then commanded to have no other Gods before Him, especially satan and his deceitful lies.

Fredric Piepenbrok and David Menebroeker

Those Babylonian churches and peoples, with the tares of satan, that are steeped in the devils deceptions and lies will undoubtedly worship him until he is truly exposed and bound at the true Christ's coming (Rev. 20:1-3) Sadly the prophets and Gods Word have always historically been ignored, despised, and ridiculed, and so too the witnesses of this time.

CHAPTER 12

Unidentified Flying Objects

Now what is this subject doing in here? Well we are dealing with truth, and lies, and deceptions, and this is one of the worlds biggest. If it is all a lie or false perception then why is it so persistently prominent and documented? If it is a truth, and they do exist, then how do they fit into the word of God and His purpose?

First are the phenomena true at all? They are present in ancient depiction of almost every culture and most definitely in our modern age of air travel. They have been witnessed in modern times by everyone from the president of Mexico, and his anta rage, to the unheard of and ignored peasants of our societies. They have, however, been witnessed by military and police personnel who are trained in observation and deduction. They have been photographed by the Hubble Scientific Telescope and tracked on both civilian and military radar. Commercial and military pilots are familiar with them to be sure.

So what does the Bible have to say about them? Nothing directly, but ask yourself what is described in the ancient writings that are given in 2 Kings 2:11; "Then it happened as they continued on and talked, that suddenly a chariot (Hebrew = "Rekeb" = a vehicle, upper millstone as riding on the lower) of fire (Hebrew = " 'Esh" = burning, firey, flaming) appeared with horses (Hebrew = "Cuwc" = to skip or leap like a horse or crane or swallow) of fire, and separated the two of them, and Elijah went up by a whirlwind (Hebrew = "Ca'ar" = tempest or whirlwind) into heaven (Hebrew = "Shamayim" = to be lofty, the sky). Obviously he was physically taken up into the sky by a vehicle of some kind of fiery power.

How did the angels, who left their proper domain, physically get here to physically impregnate the daughters of men in Gen. 6? The flood of Noah was to wipe those offspring out, by the way, and the angels responsible were bound in Tartarus (2Peter 2:4).

And what does it say of Christ Himself? John 20:17; "Jesus said to her do not cling to Me, for I have not yet ascended (Greek = "Anabaino" = to go up, ascend, to be born up) to My Father." And in Acts 1:9; "Now when He had spoken these things, while they watched, He was taken up, and a cloud (Greek = "Nephele" = cloudiness, used of the cloud which led the Israelites in the wilderness) received Him out of their sight. And while they looked steadfastly toward heaven as He went up, behold two men stood by them in white apparel, who said, Men of Galilee, why do you stand gazing up into heaven? This same Jesus, who was taken up from you into heaven, will so come in like manner as you saw Him go into heaven." He too physically ascended, but then, He can also just appear supernaturally as it is stated in Luke 24:36; "Now as they said these things, Jesus himself stood in the midst of them, and said to them Peace be with you. But they were terrified and frightened and supposed they had seen a spirit." In Mark 16:12 the same type of manifestation is referred to as it states; "After that, He appeared (Greek = "Phanerooin" = to render apparent, to manifest or show) in another form to two of them as they walked and went into the country."

To continue with the main thought of vehicular transportation as listed or referred to in the Bible let's go to Ezek 1:4; "Then I looked and behold, a whirlwind was coming out of the north, a great cloud with raging fire engulfing itself, and brightness all around it and radiating out of it's midst like the color of amber (Hebrew = "Chasmal" = polished brass), out of the midst of the fire." Verse 15-19; "Now as I looked at the living creatures, behold a wheel was on the earth beside each living creature with its four faces. The appearance of the wheels and their workings was, as it were, a wheel in the middle of a wheel. When they went, they went toward any one of the four directions; they did not turn aside when they went. As for the rims, they were so high they were awesome; and their rims were full of eyes, all around the four of them. When the living creatures went, the wheels went beside them; and when the living creatures were lifted up from the earth, the wheels were lifted up."

You could read any number of modern day transcripts on the description of what we now call UFO's and I'll bet the first chapter of Ezekiel could easily be substituted. The point is that we needn't be afraid or concerned about what we consider the unknown, because it is known by God, and there still is nothing new under the sun. God's purpose will indeed prevail. He even has a handle on our unidentified fears.

CHAPTER 13

God's Plan for Us

If you want the big picture with the least amount of distortion due to man's, or satan's, interference then look to the stars as depicted in the two books mentioned earlier, <u>The Glory of the Stars</u> and <u>Witness of the Stars</u>. If you want a more personal touch then look to God's Holy Days.

Leviticus 23 is where God's Holy Days are listed and again in Numbers 28 & 29. Deut 16 also has them. All three witness to their importance to God and man. They start with the weekly Sabbath or Saturday the seventh day of rest. It depicts a remembrance of the creative rest and our continuing rest in Yeshua, the Christ.

The Passover; It is a remembrance of Israel's deliverance from death in Egypt, a forerunner to

Christ's sacrifice for us as the Lamb of God. It is the exact day that Christ was sacrificed and death was defeated as he took the place of that lamb forever. It also depicts our own deliverance from death eternal through the hope of the resurrection as well.

The Sheaf Wave Offering; It is the Sunday that falls within each Feast of Unleavened Bread right after the Passover is celebrated. It is the exact day that Christ became the acceptable offering before God the Father. At that moment the high priest waved an unleavened loaf of bread and the first fruit of the early harvest as an acceptable offering to the Lord. Yeshua, the sinless (unleavened) bread of life, is also the first fruit of the harvest of souls. It is also a remembrance of the day that all of Israel stood on the shores of the Red Sea and God said to go forward in faith.

Unleavened Bread; It is a remembrance of the journey of Israel to Mount Sinai and their trials on their way. It symbolizes our journey and trials as we walk in freedom from sin, and with Yeshua, as we put the leavening of sin behind and from us.

Firstfruits or Pentecost; It is the exact day that Israel was given the Law or Torah at Mount Sinai. It was the day when the high priest would wave two leavened loaves (depicting puffed up and sinful men) before God as an acceptable offering and the exact day that the Holy Spirit was poured out on the first fruits of the smaller harvest with the bigger harvest yet in the future.

Trumpets; It is the beginning of the civil year for Israel (Judah alone honors it today) with a memorial blowing of the rams horn. It is also the beginning of the seventh month of God's calendar, with seven being the number of completeness and spiritual perfection. It is the month (Our Sept. or Oct. depending on the year) that Yeshua came to men the first time, and Trumpets is the prophetic day that He will come the second time, with the sound of the trumpet at the furthest out trump. That, in itself, defeats the notion that He may come at any time.

The Day of Atonement; This is the day when the high priest, now our Christ, makes atonement or reconciles us to God. It is a remembrance of our becoming one with God through His Christ, and prophetic for the masses who have yet to experience it. It is a day of fasting and acceptance of our weakness and frailty without the bread of life, our spiritual manna Yeshua.

Tabernacles; A seven day feast to thank God for all He has poured out upon us. The first day is the probable birthday of Yeshua, when He came to tabernacle among us and also depicts the millennial reign of a thousand years when he will again tabernacle with men but this time in truth, glory, and power, with satan bound.

The Last Great Day (the eight day of the Feast of Tabernacles); It is the day that Yeshua would have been presented before the LORD and circumcised. It is a day when the priests poured out copious amounts of water that symbolized the living waters that are poured out on mankind through Yeshua, the Christ. It will also be the day of the Great White Throne Judgement.

These are the Yehweh's Days and have been preserved by Judah and given to all of mankind to teach us the Love and Sovereignty of the Father. They all have, or most definitely will be, fulfilled in a time and way that only the Father knows but we can see and appreciate and honor Him in them by knowing and following His Son and our Savior Yeshua the Christ, who is the fulfillment of them all.

We are not bound to them in the strictness of the Pharisees (See the books of Ephesians and Galatians)who made a burden of counting and measuring, weighing and fearing, but neither are we allowed to substitute pagan and satanic lies or traditions in their place. Neither can we substitute or justify our rejection of them, or God, by misapplying the word of God. They clearly teach and lead us to the Christ, and honor the remembrance of His intervention in the people He has chosen to lead the rest of the world, so wouldn't an honoring of those Holy Days be more beneficial to us than honoring the lies of satan? God gave them to us for a reason. They are a remembrance and a pointing to His Truth.

Rev. 21:6; "It is done! I am the Alpha and the Omega, the Beginning and the End. I will give of the fountain of the water of life to him who thirsts. He who overcomes shall inherit all things, and I will be his God and he shall be My son."

Heb 13:8; "Jesus Christ is the same yesterday, today, and forever." Nowhere does He say undo what I have done, or I changed my mind, or it's all been a big mistake, let's do it over a different way.

Matt 5:18; "For assuredly, I say to you, till heaven and earth pass away, one jot or one tittle (these are the smallest dot or pen strokes in the Hebrew writing) will by no means pass from the law till all is fulfilled. Whoever therefore breaks one of the least of these commandments, and teaches men so, shall be called least in the kingdom of heaven, but whoever does and teaches them, he shall be called great in the kingdom of heaven."

Remember Romans 10:4; "For Christ is the end (Greek = "Telos" = the point aimed at, culmination and not termination) of the law for righteousness to everyone who believes." All things remain and culminate in Yeshua, to the glory of the Father, Yehweh. Have you not read what is written? It is written in Living Stone and it will end and begin on the Last Great Day. Praise GOD!

CHAPTER 14

What do we do now?

Having exposed satan's lies what is our recourse? We as one, or even many, can not change the plan of God and this is still an appointed time of satan's domination. The dream of the king of Babylon was and is a sure and true representation of mans time here on this earth and we can't change it (Daniel 2:34-45). What we can change is ourselves (Repent Rev 3:3). We can become as little children and accept the fact that we are not in charge of anything more than ourselves (Matt 18:3). We can look to the beam in our eye and then help and influence the smaller things in others lives; especially those God has given us as family and friends (Luke 6:42). We can start to see the expansion of our family and friends as we become part of the family of God (Be baptized, the Greek word "Baptizo" meaning fully submerged in water, as in Acts 2:38) which opens the whole world to us (Eph 3:15-19). We can serve the people around us as did Paul (1 Cor 9:19) through our employment, position, or even our infirmities (through the influence of the Holy Spirit given to those who obey Him, Acts 5:32, and who receive it through the laying on of hands, Acts 8:17). We can reflect Gods' true light to the world so that people can see the glory of God through our selfless efforts towards those who have less of His Truth (Matt 5:14-15). We can take that Truth and Light to this world of darkness one day and one step at a time. We can accept our place as a child of God and let Him take our burdens as He has the power and is willing (Matt 11:28-30).

If this is our course then the sailing becomes easy. We no longer are the pilot and the responsibility is placed where it belongs, in the hands of the one most qualified. We can enjoy the ride knowing the destination is sure and the place we are going is glorious.

We no longer have only a hope based on the sinking lies of a self appointed pilot of error but an assurance that is made sure through the facts of God's Truth and His piloting Christ.

This is the narrow course that leads to Life Eternal (Matt 7:13-14) but here it also leads to persecution

(2 Tim 3:12) and war by, and with, satan (Rev 13:7). We become the elect of God (Col 3:12) and are His forefront arm in the battle against satan in these last days. We stand clothed in the armor of God and with the sword of His Word (Eph 6:11-18) but in a servant's position (Matt 20:26-27) and not as an arrogant army (Rev 19:19). We await the true power of God at the coming of our King when Yeshua puts satan in his place of restraint so that God's way will no longer be impeded (Rev 20:2-3).

What we won't do is end up in a building with a large congregation gathered to keep and perpetuate the lies of the god of this world. We won't call on any other name than that of Yeshua or Yahweh (Zech 13:9). We won't bow to any other authority because of tradition or instruction (Col 2:8). The Word of God is our authority and it tells us to be under and subject to the worlds governing (Rom 13:8) while coming out of its spiritual domination (Rev 18:4).

A word study on the words authority, elect, light, servant, baptized, laying on of hands, little children, and repent as used in this chapter would both enhance their meaning and their usage as applied to our lives in this time. The leaders of the people of God during the Christ's time searched the scriptures but never believed or came to Him (John 5:39-40). If we are drawn as His elect (John 6:44) we must believe both what is written and who it is written for and about. We must correctly divide the scriptures with scripture (2 Peter 1:20) and as we are given we must freely give (Matt 10:8). We must come to the Christ through obedience to His Word and He will by no means cast us out (John 6:37) but give us rest (Matt 11:28) A millennial rest and an eternal rest.

We want to thank you for taking the time to read through this work and we hope your eyes and ears have been open to its truth. For your efforts may "The Lord bless you and keep you; The Lord make His face shine upon you, and be gracious to you; The Lord lift up His countenance upon you, and give you peace" (Num. 6:24-26). Amen.

ADDENDUM

Books Refered To In Text And Suggested As Further Reading And Study:

1: Biblical Mathematics Keys To Scripture Numerics By Vevangelist Ed. F. Vallowe

2: The Companion Bible The Authorized Version Of 1611 With Structures And Critical, Explanatory Notes And With 198 Appendixes By Kregel Publications

3: The Glory Of The Stars A Study Of The Zodiac By E. Raymond Capt

4: The Witness Of The Stars By E.w. Bullinger

5: Tracing Our Ancestors By Frederick Haberman

6: Great Pyramid Its Devine Message By D. Davidson And H. Aldersmith

7: The Phoenician Origin Of Britons Scots And Anglo Saxons Discovered By Phoenician And Sumerian Inscriptions In Britain By Pre Roman Briton Coins By L. Austine Waddell

8: Miracle Of The Ages The Great Pyramid By Worth Smith

9: Stonehenge And Druidism By E. Raymond Capt

10: The United States And Britain In Prophecy By Herbert W. Armstrong

11: Celebrating Biblical Feasts In Your Home Or Church By Martha Zimmerman

12: Jesus Among Other Gods By Ravi Zacharias

13: The Traditions Of Glastonbury By E. Raymond Capt

14: Complete Jewish Bible An English Version By David H. Stern And Jewish New Testament Publications, Inc.

15: Jewish New Testament Commentary By David H. Stern

16: Strong's Exhaustive Concordance Of The Bible By James Strong

17: Pilgrims Progress Personified By Fredric W. Piepenbrok

18: Book List Of Shepherds Chapel Of Gravette Arkansas

LaVergne, TN USA
11 November 2010
204550LV00001B/4/P